"I don't know you, Noem," Lavinia confessed.

"And I certainly don't want to jump into something I might regret later," she added.

"Understood."

Knowing it would be an arrangement in name only, Noem considered retreating. But since he'd come this far, he decided to press ahead. Between them, they'd have three *youngies*. Surely that would be enough to build a life on.

"I know I can't replace Josiah. Nor would I ever try. And I don't want you to be uncomfortable. You will have your own room—and plenty of privacy."

"Danke." Rocking gently, Lavinia returned her attention to the infant in her arms. Framed by the soft light emanating from the hearth, a wistful expression caressed her features.

Lifting her head, Lavinia drew back her shoulders. "After Josiah passed, I prayed *Gott* would show me where my life would go next," she said softly. "I can't explain how I know it, but I believe *Gott* sent these *kinder* for me to care for."

"Then will you be my wife?"

After a brief hesitation, she tightened her hold on his hand.

"Ja," she said in a dulcet tone. "I will."

Pamela Desmond Wright grew up in a small, dusty Texas town. Like the Amish, Pamela is a fan of the simple life. Her childhood includes memories of the olden days: old-fashioned oil lamps, cooking over an authentic wood-burning stove and making popcorn over a crackling fire at her grandparents' cabin. The authentic log cabin Pamela grew up playing in was donated to the Muleshoe Heritage Center in Muleshoe, Texas, where it is on public display.

Books by Pamela Desmond Wright

Love Inspired

The Cowboy's Amish Haven
Finding Her Amish Home
The Amish Bachelor's Bride

Visit the Author Profile page at LoveInspired.com.

The Amish Bachelor's Bride

Pamela Desmond Wright

LOVE INSPIRED
INSPIRATIONAL ROMANCE

LOVE INSPIRED®
INSPIRATIONAL ROMANCE

Recycling programs
for this product may
not exist in your area.

ISBN-13: 978-1-335-58627-8

The Amish Bachelor's Bride

Copyright © 2023 by Kimberly Fried

For questions and comments about the quality of this book, please contact us at CustomerService@Harlequin.com.

Love Inspired
22 Adelaide St. West, 41st Floor
Toronto, Ontario M5H 4E3, Canada
www.LoveInspired.com

Printed in U.S.A.

Whoso findeth a wife findeth a good thing,
and obtaineth favour of the Lord.
—*Proverbs* 18:22

This book is dedicated to my street team and beta readers. I am grateful for the support and encouragement each member gives me.

Special thanks to my editor, Melissa Endlich, and my agent, Tamela H. Murray.
I would not want to walk my journey as an author without them to guide and encourage me.

Chapter One

Humble, Wisconsin
Present day

The sky was leaden, the day as cold and overcast as Noem Witzel felt inside. Chilly fingers of a gusty spring wind tugged at his long coat, drawing its folds away from his body. Barely aware of his surroundings, he watched the cemetery workers lower the coffin into its place deep in the ground. The bishop stood at the head of the grave, reading a passage from the Bible.

The wind kicked up, caressing the nape of his neck. Shivering, Noem drew the little girl standing beside him closer to shield her from the elements. Bundled in a coat and mittens and holding a stuffed bear in one arm, his four-year-old niece sniffled. Bewildered by the loss of her *mamm*, she clutched his hand for dear life. It was too early in the morning for *youngies* to be out, but it was the only time the bishop was available to conduct the services.

Throat tightening with emotion, he glanced to his right. His *daed*, Gabriel, stood nearby, dressed in black from head to toe. Bitter agony etched the old man's features. A few feet away, the *Englisch* woman he'd hired to bring them to the cemetery cradled a swaddled infant. Unhappy in the stranger's arms, his nephew released a piteous wail.

Noem blinked against the blur rimming his vision. Three days ago, his *schwester* had passed away. Left behind were her two small *kinder*.

Ending his prayer, the bishop closed his Bible. Bending, he scraped up a handful of soil and cast it into the grave. The dirt struck the top of the coffin, scattering atop the plain wooden surface.

"Here lies Callie Evans," he intoned. "May her soul rest in the hands of the Lord."

"Amen," the small group finished, concluding the simple service. Apart from the bishop and gravediggers, no other folks from the community were in attendance.

Following the bishop's lead, Noem also scooped up a handful of the dirt. He tossed it into the depths, as did Gabriel. Confused by the ritual, Penelope stood motionless. It hadn't yet registered that her *mamm* was gone forever.

"It's okay, Penny," he said, trying to reassure the little girl over the sound of her *bruder*'s wails. "We're going to take care of you and Jesse."

She looked at him with sad eyes. "I want to go home."

Heart squeezed by her plaintive plea, he choked back a sob.

This is going to be so hard.

"I wish you could. I know you're scared, but you're going to have to live with me and your *groossdaadi* now."

Lips quivering, Penelope dropped her head. Her grip on the stuffed bear she held tightened. "Is Mamma coming soon?"

Despair twisted his insides. Feeling as if he'd been attacked by a beast from a dark place, he attempted to keep his emotions in check. "No. She isn't."

Miserable and shivering, Penelope buried her face in the faux fur toy. "I want Mamma." A sob racked her body.

Noem said nothing. Now wasn't the time. Later, he would sit down and try to explain why she'd never see her *mamm* again.

Done with his part, Bishop Graber walked

up. He was a plain-faced balding man, and sympathy etched his expression. "My condolences on your loss."

"Danke," Noem said, reverting to *Deitsch.* "I appreciate you allowing Callie to be buried beside our *mamm.*"

"Callie has passed, and so have her sins. Even though she was excommunicated, my job isn't to judge her but to pass her soul to *Gott.*" As the bishop glanced at Penelope and then the bawling infant, a question mark formed on his face. "It is a shame she leaves two *youngies* behind. Will you raise them?"

Noem tightened his grip on his niece's hand. A tragic turn of fate had landed Callie's *kinder* squarely in his care. Until he'd taken custody of the little ones, he did not know she'd even had a second *boppli.* Though he knew about Penelope, he'd never laid eyes on her. No one in the *familie* had seen Callie in person since she was nineteen. Five years ago, she'd eloped with her *Englisch* boyfriend. As she'd been baptized, their relationship was *verboten.* But Callie abandoned her faith for love. Under the rules of the *Ordnung,* she was shunned.

"Ja. I will."

The bishop glanced at the *Englisch* woman trying unsuccessfully to quiet Jesse. He continued to wail, defying her efforts. "Perhaps you should think about getting these *youngies* out of this cold."

"I think he needs his diaper changed," the woman apologized, trying to explain her failure to quiet the infant.

"If you would take him and Penelope to the van, I'll be there in a moment," Noem said, directing his niece to go with the woman. By the sullen look on her face, she wasn't pleased to be pressed into babysitting, too, but he had no other choice.

The woman nodded. "Sure, I'll keep an eye. But you know watching the kids is extra on your tab. I'm not a nanny."

"Of course."

Watching the trio depart, Noem scrubbed a hand over his mouth. Exhausted beyond weariness, he bit back a moan. A thud kicked behind his temples. The headache he'd fought for days intensified. He'd barely had time to pull himself together since receiving word of Callie's passing. Hiring a van and driver to take him to Wausau, he'd picked up her *youngies*. He barely remembered the trip or arriving at the hospital where Callie had passed. Sepsis with complications from anemia, the doctors had explained. Dazed, he'd signed everything the secretary and state social worker pushed at him, taking custody of his niece and nephew.

Between the *kinder* and his stubborn father, he hadn't had a moment to catch a wink of sleep. He wanted nothing more than to collapse and lie motionless. Numb with exhaustion, he kept on his feet through sheer will.

Doubt seeded his thoughts, shredding his ability to think. On one side was the rock. On the other was the hard place. The two were grinding together, smashing him flat.

How in the world am I going to manage this?

Mopping his brow with a handkerchief, Gabriel Witzel shook his head. "Wasn't plannin' to be raising *enkelkinder* at my age."

Noem tensed, thankful the *youngies* were out of earshot. "We talked about this."

The grizzled old man frowned. "No, *sohn*, we didn't. They belong with their *Englisch* relatives."

"How can you say such a thing?" The question rolled off Noem's tongue before he even considered whether it was appropriate to argue in front of the bishop.

"I'm just speakin' the truth." Determined to have his way, Gabriel turned to the bishop. "You should be able to give counsel on the matter."

James Graber nodded. "Maybe. Maybe not."

"By my thinkin', Callie was the one who

broke her oath." Gabriel sighed as if deeply afflicted. "Is it not true that those who have gone under the *bann* are no longer Amish?"

Pushing back his black felt hat, the bishop gave his forehead a scratch. "If you're asking for my interpretation, I'd say if you're born Amish, you're always Amish. Raised in the faith, Callie's *kinder* might choose to become members of our community when they are grown."

"The *kinder* have an *Englisch daed*," Gabriel grumbled, switching to *Deitsch*. "Callie knew when she married Erik she couldn't come back to the community. She may have been born Amish, but to my mind, her *kinder* were not. Erik should be the one to take them."

The bishop nodded graciously. "You are entitled to your thoughts, Gabriel. We can agree to disagree. I know, either way, you only want what is best for the little ones."

Planting his feet firmly, Gabriel's mouth retained a frown. "I do, and my mind is made up."

Curbing his irritation, Noem cut him off. The letter he'd received from Callie just a week before her passing had revealed her heartbreak and desperation. Erik had abandoned his *familie* for another woman. Ill and alone, she'd had no choice but to reach out to her Amish relatives.

"You k-know that's not going to h-happen. Whether or not you like it, Penny and Jesse are here to stay." The words stuck to his tongue, causing him to wince. His childhood stutter returned at the most inconvenient times.

"How can we take care of them and work?" Gabriel demanded. "We both have jobs from sunup to sundown."

"I—I'll hire a live-in nanny."

"*Ach!* And just where do ye think you'll be puttin' a female?" he asked with sarcastic asperity. "Unless you plan to wed her, she can't live under our roof."

"It's going to take a few days, but I'll figure out something."

Digging in his heels, Gabriel crossed his arms. "Needs to be someone trustworthy."

"I'll do my best," Noem said, attempting to calm his agitated parent. It didn't help. The anger between them stretched on. Each had his side, and neither was backing down.

Releasing a huff through flared nostrils, Gabriel Witzel's grim expression tightened. "I want no part in the matter. This is nothin' but trouble. Mark my words." Settling his hat on his head, he strode away from the grave without a backward glance. Once he'd climbed into his buggy, he set the horse in motion. The vehicle clattered down the gravel road.

Taking shovels in hand, the gravediggers began their task in silence. No one spoke. As far as they were concerned, Callie Evans was to be shunned, even in death. It was why no one in the community had come to pay their last respects. Out of deference for her *familie*, the bishop had allowed her burial. Like most Amish cemeteries, it was located on the outskirts of town, on a piece of land dedicated for use by the community. The grounds were meticulously kept, grass and hedges trimmed. A huge marble carving of a book with the Lord's Prayer inscribed into its stone pages sat positioned between two towering weeping willow trees. There were iron benches beneath the trees, inviting the bereaved to sit beneath their shelter and seek comfort.

Noem watched his *daed* leave. Refusing to ride in the hired vehicle, Gabriel had insisted on getting himself to the funeral by the traditional Amish means of transportation. In a way, it was a relief. Being around his *daed* was getting harder and harder. Gabriel rarely smiled and only spoke when spoken to. It was as if he wanted to punish *Gott* for taking his beloved *ehefrau*. Unfortunately, the only ones the old man was punishing were the few friends and *familie* members he had left.

"I'm sorry, Bishop. I didn't mean to drag you in on our argument."

Bishop Graber placed a hand on his shoulder. "I think you're a fine man for trying to do right by the *kinder*. I'll pray your *daed* reconsiders."

"*Danke*. I need all the prayers I can get."

Sensing his turmoil, the bishop took Noem by the elbow and led him away from the grave. "You mentioned you were planning to hire a *tagesmutter* to look after the *youngies*."

Noem didn't look back. He couldn't.

"*Ja,*" he said, recalling his disastrous attempts to get the *boppli* changed and fed before leaving for the service. "I'm going to place a notice at the market and in the newspaper."

"You'll need a single woman who is *gut* with *kinder*."

"Your recommendation would be welcome."

Bishop Graber halted his steps. "I'd prefer to make a suggestion you might not have considered."

"Please do."

"What would you think of a *familie* formation arrangement?"

Noem blinked. Finding himself a wife and

getting married was the furthest thing from his mind.

"You mean take an *ehefrau*?"

"That is exactly what I am suggesting."

Taken aback, he stammered out a quick reply. "B-but I'm not s-seeing anyone."

The bishop held up a hand. "Hear me out before you say no." His expression held the intent look of a sensible man.

"I'm listening."

"I believe you know Lavinia Simmons."

"Ja," he said, forcing himself to slow down and speak with precision. "She was friends with Callie when they were in school. But that was years ago." Despite the passage of time, it was easy to picture Lavinia's face. Then, her name had been Mueller. With her coal-black hair and dark eyes, she was quite a striking teenager. A lovely girl, she had a kind nature and a generous spirit.

"You know she is a recent widow."

He nodded. "Very sad loss for her. He was so young." He'd attended Josiah's service but doubted Lavinia had known he was there. The funeral was large, and hundreds had attended. He was just another face in the crowd. Dazed with grief, she probably didn't care. As he and Josiah weren't close friends, Noem had seen no reason to bother her.

The bishop momentarily pursed thin lips. "Far be it from me to spread gossip, but Josiah left her in a bad way financially."

"I didn't know."

"Did I mention she has a *tochter*? Sophie is nearly three. Having another *youngie* around to bond with would be good for your niece."

"I suppose," Noem allowed, turning his collar up against the gusty wind. "But we barely know each other nowadays. We aren't even in the same church district. Would it be p-proper to approach her?"

"Why not? You have a home and need a *gut* woman to manage it. Why not combine your resources and raise your *youngies* together?"

Falling silent, Noem turned the idea over. His mind flitted back to a time when he'd known Lavinia better. He'd always liked her and didn't have a bad word to say against her character. During their *rumspringa*, he'd considered asking her on a date. But he'd hemmed and hawed so long that Josiah Simmons had stepped in line in front of him. Believing he'd missed his chance, he'd decided not to throw his hat in the ring after Josiah took a fancy to her. The match had worked out. The couple married soon thereafter.

Lavinia had slipped through his fingers once. Taking a wretched turn, fate now presented a second chance. She was a young widow. He had a niece and a nephew who needed a woman to help raise them.

The idea enticed him. It would be a reasonable step. Love had nothing to do with what was often a practical solution.

Mind cutting a new track, he dragged in a breath. Marry Lavinia Simmons? Given thought, it wasn't as absurd as it might seem. Though they'd lost touch in recent years, they'd always gotten along in their youth.

Would she be open to the idea?

There was only one way to find out.

Lifting the blinds of the kitchen window, Lavinia Simmons gazed over the fenced-in yard. A glance told her the day was going to be dim. A brisk wind flicked at the trees. The threat of a storm hung in the air.

She searched for a bit of cheer. April showers bring May flowers.

Looking outside, she couldn't help but think of her *ehmann*. The first stirrings of spring used to be Josiah's favorite time of the year. He'd worked hard to landscape the acreage surrounding the home he'd built with his own hands. The whitewashed house nestled amid lovingly planted gardens, where a variety of plants grew in lush abundance. After a long, frosty winter, the eager buds were beginning to raise their sleepy heads. Soon, they would burst into an array of colorful blossoms.

Spring was a renewal, a resurrection. Not only of the spirit but also of hope. Just as the Heavenly Father promised.

But this year Josiah wouldn't celebrate the coming of the new season. His eyes were forever closed, and his soul rested in the hands of the Lord. The accident that had almost taken his young nephew's life had taken Josiah's instead. Though the *youngie* was warned to stay away from the frozen pond, Eli had wandered onto the ice. Weak and not yet frozen solid, the fragile surface had given way, plunging the *kinder* into freezing water. Chopping wood nearby, Josiah heard Eli's cries and rushed to help. He'd gotten the *boi* out safely, but not before taking on a chill. Rushed to the hospital, he'd died a few hours later of respiratory system failure brought on by hypothermia. His death was sudden and unexpected.

Vision blurring, she pressed a hand to her mouth to stifle a sob. Josiah had passed last November, just before the holidays. Healthy and in the prime of life, he should have had a bright future.

But *Gott* had other plans.

"Lavinia?" Her *bruder*'s voice interrupted her thoughts. "Did you hear a word I've said?"

Swiping at her eyes, Lavinia turned away from the window. "Forgive me. My mind wandered. Give me a minute and I'll have some tea ready."

Peering over the rim of his glasses, Abram Mueller offered a smile. "Take your time. I'm still going over the paperwork that will close the mortgage and get everything out of Josiah's name."

"I'm sorry you're having to help me." Flipping on the tap, Lavinia filled a kettle with water before setting it on the stove. After adding loose tea leaves to a metal ball, she dropped it inside to steep. Stomach going tight, her hands shook. "I'm still shocked to find out he mortgaged our home without my knowledge."

Setting out her best china, she filled two delicate cups with the tarry brew. The scent of bergamot tickled her nostrils as steam rose. A hot cup of Earl Grey would be just the thing to set her right. Having added a pitcher of fresh cream and a bowl of sugar to a tray, she carried everything to the table.

Expression serious, Abram scribbled a few figures. "The property should have been in both of your names. Then he couldn't have gambled away the roof over your head."

Lavinia sat, smoothing her hands across her lap. "I wish it was all a bad dream." After his death, she'd discovered Josiah had kept a lot of secrets. Her perfect *ehmann* was a deeply flawed man.

Abram shook his head. "There would have come a point when he had to tell you he couldn't make the payments anymore."

She blinked. Barely five months had gone by since Josiah died. In that brief time, her life had fallen completely apart.

Gaze blurring again, her throat tightened. She curled her hands around the fragile cup, but its warmth did little to chase away the chill. Josiah's deceptions had transformed the calm sea of her life into a churning ocean. She was flailing, struggling to swim before she sank like a rock beneath choppy waves of doubt, despair, and loss.

"I can't believe he owed so much money," she said, voice trembling. "I keep asking myself why I never knew."

Sensing her distress, Abram laid a hand on her arm. His expression was soft with pity. "Josiah had a sickness, a disease of the mind and spirit. He was *gut* at hiding it."

Indeed, he was.

Sipping her tea, Lavinia forced herself to swallow. Josiah had an illness. All those times she'd believed he was working overtime at the mill were nights he'd spent in a den of iniquity, gambling with men of low repute who were eager to take advantage of his weakness.

Gambling, like misusing alcohol or drugs, was an addiction. Unfortunately, a weakness for sin didn't exclude the Amish. Plain folks were still human and faced the same demons of temptation. From the bits they'd gathered, Josiah's habit began during his *rumspringa*. That was the time when Amish adolescents could live like *Englischers* and try out their way of life. It encouraged youths to explore movie theaters, driving, malls and more. But some often took part in unhealthy behaviors. A new casino had opened in the neighboring town, attracting the ire of concerned citizens. It was also a magnet for those seeking something to do on a slow Saturday night.

Josiah got hooked on cards and dice. The more he lost, the harder he tried to recover the money. That only led to more losses. It was a vicious cycle he couldn't break free of. At the time of his death, he'd dug himself into debt. He'd gotten in so deep he'd missed several payments to the bank.

Teetering on the edge of bankruptcy, she'd made the heartbreaking decision to sell the house and the acreage it sat on before the lender foreclosed. In her mind, it was the honorable thing to do. After the bank was paid, the remaining money cleared the rest of Josiah's debts. He'd left a long trail of IOUs behind. More than once, a few unsavory characters had shown up, demanding payment on the markers they held. Too ashamed and afraid to report the matter to the police, she'd promised the men they would get their money. The Amish didn't like involving *Englisch* law enforcement in their business. The sooner she laid her *ehmann*'s secret shame to rest, the sooner she could move on.

Unfortunately, selling the house left her and Sophie without a roof over their heads. Amish houses were highly valued. An *Englisch* couple had quickly snapped up the deal. Now that everything was finalized and the money from the sale transferred into the proper hands, she had two weeks to vacate.

All she had was her daughter, the clothes on her back and a few personal possessions. The last seven years of her life had been completely wiped away. It was hard not to be angry at Josiah. But holding on to her resentment wouldn't do any good. The only thing she could do was pray for his soul, forgive him and move on.

As for Josiah's *familie*... They'd refused to believe he had a problem and had turned their backs on her. The rejection hurt but wasn't entirely unexpected. As the only *sohn*, Josiah could do no wrong. In their eyes, she was the one to blame for allowing him to build a fine house he couldn't afford.

A small voice interrupted.

"Mamma?"

Lavinia perked up. Having risen at dawn, she'd not wanted to wake her *tochter*, preferring to let her sleep. Sophie was such a fussy child at bedtime. In her mind, the mattress was an enemy, and she'd rather play than sleep. Getting her to lie down and rest was a daily battle.

Abram offered his niece a smile. "*Gut* morning, my *sonnenschein*."

Face flushed, Sophie padded across the warm kitchen. "Not you." She pouted as her little feet pummeled the floor.

Lavinia set her daughter in her lap. "Be polite to your *onkel* Abram," she scolded.

"I'm hungry." Gaze webbed with sleep, Sophie rubbed her eyes. "I want jammy bread."

Lavinia kissed her daughter's forehead. "I'll fix it in a minute. Now mind your manners."

"I see my niece is cranky today." After pushing aside the binder, Abram took off his glasses and pinched the bridge of his nose. "Have you given any more thought to my offer?"

Lavinia shook her head. "I couldn't move in on top of you and Maddie. That wouldn't be fair."

"Why not? Instead of adding two more rooms to Gran'pa's house, we can make it three."

Touched by his gracious offer, she glanced at her older *bruder*, now heavily bearded since his marriage. Thick dark curls covered his cheeks and chin, concealing the scars of a childhood accident. A kind, good-hearted man, Abram never failed to step up and help when trouble knocked.

"You and Maddie are still newlyweds and have *twins on the way*," she said, shaking her head. "You already have enough on your hands."

"Which is why we're remodeling to add a *dawdy haus* for Gran'pa Amos and extra bedrooms. We can easily change the plans. We could even turn the basement into a nice little apartment for you and Sophie if you don't want to live in the main house."

"It just wouldn't feel right," she said, wishing he understood her feelings. "I'm used to having my own home. Not being the poor relation who needs a handout."

"That's what *familie* does." Abram reached for her arm, squeezing it. "We help each other.

And Rolf, Samuel, Annalise and Elam would all make a place for you in their homes, too. They have all offered, I know."

Lavinia hugged her *youngie* tighter. "They have. But it's not what I want."

Abram drew his hand away. "Then what are you planning to do?"

"I'm not sure. I've been asking the Lord to show me which way I should go." She tipped her head. "Isn't that what we are supposed to do, Minister? Let *Gott* tackle our woes?"

His gaze softened. "Nothing is impossible with *Gott*."

"I know." Standing, she lifted Sophie into her high chair. "Excuse me while I make breakfast."

Though she'd pulled out her skillet and set it atop the stove, she had no chance to continue cooking. The doorbell sent out a melodious chime.

She frowned. *Who could that be?* She was not expecting any more company that day.

Smoothing her apron and straightening her *kapp*, Lavinia hurried to the front door. Surely it wasn't the new owners. If they had their way, she and Sophie would already be sitting on the curb with cardboard boxes to hold their things.

Englischers *are so pushy. They have no patience.*

Throwing open the door, she recognized Bishop Graber. Dressed in a black suit, he was his usual natty self. Beard laced with gray, his thick-framed glasses sat firmly on his nose.

"Guten morgen," he greeted, tipping his hat. "I've someone who'd like to speak with you."

Lavinia's gaze turned to the bishop's companion. Holding the hand of a small frizzy-haired girl, he awkwardly cradled an infant in the crook of his elbow. Tall and broad-shouldered, he was also clad in black attire. Blond curls sneaked out from beneath the brim of his felt hat. Cheeks covered with stubble, he had wide-set eyes, a straight nose and a gently cleft chin. Eyes puffy and red, his face was pale and drawn. By the look of him, he was down, out and exhausted.

Recognition seeped into her memory. "Noem? Noem Witzel?" Though they didn't run in the same social circle nowadays, his *schwester* had once been a dear friend.

A nod. *"Ja."*

Perplexed, she looked to the little ones accompanying him. "I didn't know you had a *familie.*"

"The *youngies* aren't his," Bishop Graber said, taking it upon himself to explain. "They belong to Callie, and she can't care for them anymore."

Gaze roaming their somber attire and expressions, Lavinia felt the blood drain from her face. "What's happened?"

Noem briefly pursed his lips. Sorrow haunted his eyes. "I hate to say it, but she's passed away."

Chapter Two

Shaken, Lavinia felt a shiver circle her spine. When she'd opened the door, it wasn't the sort of news she'd expected from visitors. Though she'd fallen out of touch with Callie, she'd wondered now and again how her friend's life had turned out after she'd given up her ties to the church and gone *Englisch*.

By the look of things, it hadn't gone well.

Knowing how close they'd once been, she imagined Noem wanted to drop by and tell her in person. She and Callie had grown up together. They'd met on the first day of school and became fast friends. Joined at the hip, they'd spent many a weekend on sleepovers, planning their lives and picking out cute boys they wanted to marry. It didn't seem right a woman so full of life and laughter had been taken away from her *youngies*.

Pulling her thoughts together, Lavinia stepped back. "Come in, please," she said, ushering the small group out of the icy wind.

Hurrying inside, Noem did his best to shield the infant swaddled in blankets. Jostled, the unhappy *boppli* squalled at the top of his lungs.

"He's been fussing all morning."

Lavinia set her hands on her hips. "*Ach*, shame on you for dragging an infant out into the cold." Clucking her tongue, she immediately held out her arms. "Hand him to me."

"*Danke*. His name is Jesse."

"Jesse. Such a nice name." Pressing the *boppli* against her shoulder, Lavinia patted his back with the flat of her hand. "There, there. No need for tears." Calmed by her touch, the infant stopped bawling. Burrowing his head in the crook of her neck, he quit his fussing.

"How did you do that?"

"A *boppli* knows when you don't know how to handle them." Catching sight of the small girl, she gave an inquisitive look. "And I see you have another. Who is this *kleiner*?"

Noem nudged his niece forward. "Penelope. She's shy." The expression on the little girl's face warred between fear and confusion.

"My, she's so pretty." Lavinia couldn't even imagine how scared Penelope must feel. No wonder the little *mädchen* looked so unhappy and withdrawn.

"I hope we're not intruding," the bishop continued, taking off his hat.

She shook her head. "Not at all, Bishop. I was just going over a few things with Abram. Please, have a seat. Could I get you some coffee or tea?"

"*Danke*. Tea will do for me." Once he'd hung his coat, the bishop headed toward the table.

"*Gut* to see you, Bishop," Abram said, rising from his chair. The two men shook hands, greeting each other cordially. Stepping forward, Abram also offered his hand to Noem. "Have you just come from the service?"

"*Ja*. Callie was laid to rest this morning."

"Had I known, I would have attended to pay my respects."

Lavinia nodded. "Me, too."

"I appreciate that," Noem said and swallowed hard. "But I wouldn't have expected it since she was under the *bann*. The bishop allowed her to be interred in the *familie* plot."

James Graber plunked himself in a chair. "The things we have done in this world pass with us when we die. I would not hold any judgment against Callie. Neither should anyone else."

"Amen," Abram murmured.

Tightening her grip on the wriggling infant, Lavinia snuggled him closer. Her sympathies went out to both motherless *kinder*.

"My heart ached when she left the community. I'd always hoped she would find her way home and we could be friends again."

"I'm sorry, too." Noem slipped a baby bag off his shoulder and then helped Penelope out of her coat before taking off his own. He hung them on the peg beside the back door. "I apologize for bringing our trouble to your home."

Lavinia offered a smile. "No trouble. I'm glad you came by."

Seeing Sophie perched in her baby chair, Penelope immediately made her way to the younger girl.

"How pretty," she said, reaching out to touch one of the bows attached to the toddler's braids. "I like pink."

Lavinia eyed Penelope's tangles. "Well, you shall have some bows, too. When I have a moment, I'll comb your hair." She turned a narrow stare on Noem. "Whoever has been looking after these *youngies* has been neglectful."

"That would be me," he said, and then explained. "I've only had them a couple of days. I haven't had a chance to go back to Wausau and get their things, so I haven't got much to work with."

"I see." Schooling her face into a neutral expression, she nodded toward her *tochter.* "I was just about to feed Sophie. Would you care to join us?"

"I'm not hungry, but I'm sure the *kinder* are."

Growing angsty over his empty tummy, the *boppli* released another cry.

Lavinia patted his diapered bottom. "I think he's saying he'd like to be fed."

Noem dug in the diaper bag. "I have his things," he said, producing a bottle half full of formula. "I've been having trouble getting him to eat it."

Claiming the bottle, Lavinia sat down. "This is the best way to get a *boppli* to take a bottle." Positioning the infant's head in the crook of her arm, she wrapped her hand around his bottom before lifting her elbow so that his head was at a slight angle. "Now place the nipple on his lips and give them a little tickle. When he starts to root, pop it in his mouth." Demonstrating, she gave the infant's mouth a little pressure with the tip. Jesse instantly latched on, nursing with gusto. His plump lips worked hard to draw the milk down.

"You make it look easy."

Tipping the bottle away, Lavinia temporarily halted the flow. "Now make sure he's not nursing too fast, or he'll get a bellyache." Easing the bottle back into place, she allowed the infant to resume. "It's just a matter of patience."

Noticing her sibling getting all the attention, Penelope turned up an imploring face. "Can I have something?"

"Of course," Lavinia said, checking Jesse's progress. "Your *bruder* should be full."

Abram held out his hands. "I'll burp him. I could use the practice since I've got twins on the way."

"Danke." Lavinia stood. She gave the infant to Abram, and then brushed a few wrinkles out of her apron. "Do you like scrambled eggs and jam bread?" she asked Penelope.

Caressing Sophie's silky dark locks, Penelope nodded with shy enthusiasm. "Yes, please."

Taking command of her kitchen, Lavinia gathered the ingredients and set to cooking.

"Can I help?" Noem asked.

"Pour the bishop and yourself a cup of tea," she directed, cracking a few eggs into a bowl and whipping them into a froth.

Nodding, he followed her instruction, filling two cups. He carried both to the table and handed the bishop one.

"Danke." James Graber added cream and sugar to his cup.

After finishing the eggs, Lavinia divided the portions between two small plates. She sliced thick pieces of bread and toasted each side lightly before adding a thick smear of butter and berry jam. Pouring milk into a small cup and a sippy cup, she nodded toward the sofa in the living room.

"Take a cushion and set it under Penelope," she instructed. "Then she can eat at the table like a big girl."

Doing as instructed, Noem placed his niece at the table. "There you go."

Satisfied, Lavinia served the girl her meal. "This will fill your tummy."

Sitting quietly, Penelope didn't move.

Noem frowned helplessly. "What's wrong?"

"Mamma says we can't eat until we thank Jesus."

"Do you know how to say grace?" the bishop asked.

Penelope gave a vigorous nod. "I can."

"Then we will bow our heads while you say your prayer," James Graber said.

Closing her eyes, Penelope pressed her palms together. "For all food yummy that fills my tummy. Thank You, God. Amen!" Prayer done, she claimed her spoon and dug into the food as if she'd never eaten a decent meal.

James Graber smiled. "That's a fine prayer."

"I'll teach it to my *youngies* when they are old enough to learn." Repositioning Jesse against his shoulder, Abram patted his back with the flat of his hand.

The infant let out a loud burp. "Gaaa." Waving plump hands in the air, he gurgled with contentment.

"That's what we needed. Better a burp than down and out." Claiming Jesse, Lavinia gave his diaper a quick check. Finished with her meal, Sophie kicked to be let down.

Abram rose and wrung out a washcloth to clean his niece's hands and face, and then placed her on her feet. "Why don't you show Penelope some of your toys?"

Sophie nodded eagerly. Enticed by the idea, Penelope slipped out of her chair. Hand in hand, they headed into the living room to play with a set of hand-carved animals based on those in Noah's ark.

Satisfied the *youngies* were out from underfoot, Lavinia cleaned up the kitchen. Stepping up, Noem dried the dishes with quiet efficiency. Reaching for a plate, his hand bumped hers.

"You don't have to help."

"I don't m-mind," he murmured, giving her a shy smile.

Warmed by his gentle nature, she felt a blush

creep into her face. A hitch stalled her breath. Years had passed since she'd last spent time in his company. She'd forgotten what a fine-looking fellow he was. The awkward teen she remembered had grown into a handsome man. How is it she'd never noticed his eyes were a peculiar shade of green mixed with brown? Hazel. That was the color. So unusual.

Sipping his tea, the bishop glanced at the binder Abram had set aside. The bill of sale for the house and acreage lay atop it. "You've sold the house?"

Glancing at Noem, Lavinia considered her reply. Aside from Abram and a few other close *familie* members, only Bishop Graber knew the truth about the mess Josiah had made of their finances. People would find out soon enough she'd let the property go, but it was no one's business why.

"Ja," she said, deciding not to skirt the matter. "To a nice *Englisch* couple."

"It's a beautiful place," Noem said, looking around. "Why would you want to leave?"

Not exactly a question she wanted to answer honestly.

"Now that Josiah's gone, I couldn't bear to stay." That much was true. Discovering she'd lived under the same roof as the man who'd deceived her disturbed her. She wasn't sure what to make of Josiah's double life. On one hand, he'd professed himself to be a *Gott*-fearing Christian. He went to church on Sundays and often took part in community programs. People liked him. Respected him. Trusted him.

Yet he'd fooled them all. Had lied to everyone's faces even as he'd wrapped himself in the cloak of a *gut* and pious man.

Her *ehmann*'s deceptions were gut-twisting. Selling the house and walking away was the only way she could wipe away the past, cleanse herself for the part she'd played in his lies. Ever the supportive wife, she'd defended Josiah when members of her *familie* had questioned his habit of falling out of touch for hours. Because gambling didn't have the usual physical health signs of serious addiction, it was easy for him to conceal his habit.

Noem's gaze sharpened. "Where will you go?"

Abram leaned forward. "I've invited her to live with me and Maddie and Gran'pa Amos. The more, the merrier, I always say."

Bouncing lightly as she held Jesse, Lavinia shook her head. "As much as I love my *bruder*, I am not about to take him up on the offer."

Finishing his tea, James Graber lowered his cup. "Then perhaps you will hear me out. I have a solution you might find most suitable."

Brow crinkling, Abram gave his beard a pensive scratch. "I'm not one to jump to conclusions, but I believe I know why you and Noem are here. Correct me if I am wrong."

"Ja." Peering over the edge of his glasses, the older man mantled himself in the authority of his position. "It is my recommendation Noem and Lavinia would do well to marry."

Cup in hand, Noem sat on the living room sofa. Nerves on edge, he fortified his exhausted body with caffeine. Even though he longed for sleep, his mind kept revving. A multitude of thoughts crowded his brain. So much had happened since he'd received word of Callie's passing. Her life was in disarray when she'd fallen ill. As her closest relative, he was the only one left to pick up the pieces.

Drawing a breath, he tried to relax by concentrating on the sound of rain drumming on the roof. The gray day had turned into a storm, throwing down a torrent.

Blinking hard, he glanced toward Lavinia. Her wide dark eyes, full lips and swanlike neck gave her a look of wholesomeness. Beneath the crispness of her gaze was a suggestion of daring, intelligence and vulnerability. A pretty girl, she'd matured into a beautiful woman. The kind of woman a man would be proud to have on his arm. She sat with Jesse, rocking in a chair near the hearth. For some reason, the infant had turned fussy and seemed uncomfortable.

"Is something wrong with him?"

Lavinia lifted the infant to her shoulder. Patting his back with a firm hand, she spoke in soft words. "He's not crying or stiff, so I don't think it's colic. I would say it's because he's off his schedule. Everything's unfamiliar, and he's not used to strange folks handling him."

Noem's gaze raked the little fellow. "You're probably right. How's he supposed to know we're trying to take care of him?"

"*Ach*, he knows there's been a change in his life. Nothing has the feel of home, and the touch he knew from his *mamm* is gone. We can try to duplicate it, but it isn't the same. We don't look, smell or speak the way Callie did, nor can we. Until he gets used to different handling, he'll be fussy."

"I had no idea a *kind* knew anything. I thought all they did was eat, sleep and make a lot of smelly diapers."

A chuckle slipped past her lips. "Oh, they do more than that. They teach us to be gentle and to open our hearts." Lowering Jesse, she gave a warm smile as she gently rocked him to sleep. "*Kinder* are a gift from *Gott*."

"How long do you think it will take them to get used to the changes?"

"A month. Maybe more. Once the *kinder* are in a normal routine, they'll adapt to their new home. A schedule will help keep order and focus in their day."

He shook his head. "I wasn't p-prepared to be raising two little ones."

"Sometimes what we expect to get in life and what it hands us are two different things. *Gott* willed that Callie be taken," she said, falling back on the stoic and reserved approach most Amish took when dealing with the passing of a loved one. "We may not like the Lord's decision, but we must accept it."

"So many in my *familie* have passed. I'm not sure if anyone's really in control. Maybe it's just some cosmic joke the universe plays on us poor humans."

"*Gott* knows how things should work in our lives. We must be patient and trust He will give us the answers we seek."

Speaking of answers…

Over an hour had passed since Bishop Graber explained the reason behind their visit. Lavinia had listened closely, as had Abram. But she'd yet to voice an opinion on the matter.

"You haven't given me a reply," Noem said,

nudging her back to the subject that hung between them.

"About the bishop's suggestion?"

"*Ja*. What do you think?"

Lavinia glanced across the room. The bishop and her *bruder* sat at the kitchen table, speaking in quiet tones.

Noem followed her gaze. "The decision isn't theirs. It's yours."

Releasing a soft sigh, she shook her head. Sorrow flickered in her gaze. "Josiah's not been in the grave long. I'm not sure I'm ready to commit myself to another so soon."

Gaze scraping over her, he couldn't fail to notice she looked pale and tired. Stress was apparent, showing in the small crinkles around the corners of her eyes and the edges of her mouth. By the look of conflict warring within her expression, he knew losing her *ehmann* was a tragedy that had torn her life into shreds.

"Understandable. We haven't s-seen each other in years. Having me show up on your doorstep with two *youngies* is a lot to think about in one day."

Lavinia patted his nephew's back softly, lulling the infant into releasing a low coo. Settling down, he was close to falling into a restful sleep. "Callie's *kinder* are adorable," she allowed. "I'm honored you would choose me to help raise them."

"You are the only one I'd consider." Attempting to be more persuasive, he added, "I make a *gut* living. You and Sophie would want for nothing." Knowing she'd had to sell her house and would be dependent on the kindness of *familie* and friends only redoubled his determination to offer a solution that would allow her to keep her dignity. They needed each other. He just had to convince her he could offer a solid foundation to build a future on.

Myriad emotions flickered across Lavinia's expressive face before she offered a reply.

"If we were to wed, you would expect me to be a wife. *Ja?*"

The question brought him up short. The notion hadn't crossed his mind. Her concern was valid.

Embarrassed by the delicate subject, he tugged at his collar before clearing his throat. "Is it s-something you would want?"

"I could only be with a man I loved," she confessed. "I like you, Noem. At least, I like the young man I knew back then. But I don't know you now. And I certainly don't want to jump into something I might regret later."

"Understood."

"Josiah is the only man I expected to spend

my life with. Losing him—" Her throat worked with emotion. "I don't know if I have it in me to give my heart away a second time."

Knowing theirs would be a coupling in name only, Noem considered retreating. But doing so would leave him stuck back at square one. As he'd come this far, he decided to press ahead. Between them, they'd have three *youngies*. That would be quite a handful. Surely that would be enough.

"I know I can't replace Josiah. Nor would I ever try. And I don't want you to be uncomfortable if you decide to accept Bishop Graber's recommendation. You will have a room to yourself—and plenty of privacy."

"Danke." Rocking gently, Lavinia returned her attention to the infant in her arms. Framed by the soft light emanating from the hearth, a wistful expression caressed her features. "Such a handsome *boi*. Josiah and I prayed we'd have a *sohn*."

Sensing longing in her tone, Noem perked up. "Jesse could be your *sohn*. And Penelope could be Sophie's *schwester*. I have full guardianship. We could petition the court to adopt them, make them our own."

Curiosity claimed her expression. "Where is their *daed*? Why does he not have them?"

Noem inwardly winced. He'd sidestepped a

few details of Callie's life. Most of it was done out of deference for Penelope. His niece didn't need to overhear anything negative about her parents. Glancing toward the play area, he saw she and Sophie were engrossed in the simple games Lavinia had provided to entertain them.

"Erik left Callie when he found out she was going to have Jesse. According to the letter I received from her, they'd been having problems. He wasn't happy about another *kind*. He'd also met another woman and filed for d-divorce. Based on what Callie wrote, Erik wants nothing to do with them." Frustrated, he spread his hands. "I—I haven't had time to go through Callie's things to find the paperwork or a contact number."

"I can't image how Callie must have felt."

Anger bubbled up. "When she started seeing Erik, I warned her he would be trouble. I never liked the fellow."

"I remember when she met him," Lavinia said, frowning. "She fell head over heels. Dark hair, dark eyes and that sporty car of his were all she saw."

"I've thought about contacting Erik's *familie*. But I doubt they would want to raise Penelope and Jesse. Callie could have reached out to them when she got sick, but she chose not to. Since it was shaping up to be an ugly d-divorce, I imagine they took Erik's side in the matter. It doesn't look like he was paying any sort of support, either. As for finding him—" A shrug rolled off his shoulders. "He walked away from Callie and the *kinder*. Even if I could locate him, I don't think he'd be a fit parent."

Lashes fluttering, Lavinia swiped at her eyes. "Had I known Callie had fallen so low, I would have reached out to her. I know she was under the *bann*, but I could have sent things for her and the *kinder*. Others who knew her would have, too. No one would let one of our own go without necessities."

"Callie's letter came just a few days before she passed. She told me everything that had happened since she left. She said she'd been sick and needed help. I overnighted some money. And I'd planned to make a trip to Wausau to check on things when I got some time off work." As if he was defeated by the narrative, his shoulders sagged. "But it was too little, too late. She collapsed and had to be rushed to the hospital. The doctor said she didn't live long after they got her to the ER."

Having fallen to silence as Noem and Lavinia conversed, Bishop Graber and Abram gave them both an expectant look. The men rose and walked into the living room.

"Have you settled on an agreement?" the bishop asked.

"You do know each other. And you each have a need the other can ease," Abram added.

Lavinia glanced between the two church elders. "You believe it would be an acceptable solution?"

"Ja," Abram confirmed and then continued. "I would not recommend it if Noem were a stranger, but you grew up together. Starting with friendship, you two could build a life together."

"And courtship is a private matter," James Graber said. "No one outside of this room need know how long you have been considering the notion."

Visibly taking a breath, Lavinia lowered her gaze. The chair she sat in rocked back and forth with a gentle motion. Adjusting the blankets around the *boppli*, she gave his chubby cheeks a soft caress. Unaware of the turmoil surrounding him, the little *boi* slept securely in her loving embrace.

Noem felt his breath stall. No matter what she had to say, his entire life was about to undergo a major change. Whether he would walk the path alone hinged on her reply.

A quiet moment ticked away. And then another.

Lifting her head, she drew back her shoulders. "After Josiah passed, I prayed *Gott* would show me where my life would go next," she said softly. "For the longest time, I've felt lost." As she glanced at the infant slumbering peacefully in her arms, her turbulent expression smoothed. "I can't explain how I know it, but I believe *Gott* sent these *kinder* for me to care for."

"Then you will agree?" Bishop Graber asked, looking quite satisfied his matchmaking had met with success.

"Callie was my friend. I can honor her memory by ensuring Penelope and Jesse are raised in a *gut* Amish home. I believe she would do nothing less for Sophie if our circumstances were reversed." Her words, simply spoken, were heartfelt and heartwarming.

Encouraged, Noem rose. Going to one knee, he dared to reach for her hand. She didn't pull away when his fingers gently closed around hers.

"Will you be my wife?"

Lids dropping to shield her gaze, Lavinia bit her lower lip. A faint tremble revealed her uncertainty. After a brief hesitation, she tightened her hold on his hand.

"Ja," she said in a dulcet tone. "I will."

Chapter Three

Three days later...

Jarred from sleep by bright shards of light dancing across her face, Lavinia opened her eyes. Rubbing away the remnants of sleep, she checked the windup clock at her bedside. Twenty after seven.

She normally rose before the sun, but last night she'd tossed and turned for hours. Her mind refused to let her rest, revving into overdrive as she considered the consequences of her hasty decision.

She'd agreed to marry Noem Witzel.

And today was the day of their wedding.

Doubt immediately set in, attacking with a vengeance. Emotions flooded from all sides, filling her mind with a jumble of images. Learning of her friend's death, she'd felt compelled to help care for Callie's innocent *youn-*

gies. But agreeing to marry Callie's brother? Pure foolishness!

Her hand lifted, pressing against her mouth as the stark realization set in.

What have I done?

Anxious and out of sorts, she threw off the covers and slipped out of bed. She belted her robe around her waist. The hour was early. There was still time to contact Bishop Graber and call off the ceremony that was scheduled to take place after the Sunday morning service. If she dressed and hurried to the phone shanty, she could make the call.

Scurrying into the adjoining bathroom, she washed her face and dressed for the day. Hair half done, she doffed her *kapp*. Didn't matter if it was crooked or if the strings hung. No one would care so early in the morning.

Leaving her room, she headed to Sophie's room to check the *kinder*. She'd agreed to keep Penelope and Jesse with her because Noem needed time to arrange the Witzel home to accommodate four new occupants. He also needed time to retrieve their belongings from Callie's place in Wausau. As he couldn't transport the items in a buggy, a van would have to be hired. It made sense she would take over caring for the *youngies* while Noem took care of his *schwester*'s business. She was to be the children's surrogate *mamm*. The sooner they got used to her, the better. And once she'd wed Noem, her belongings would need to be picked up and moved.

Cracking open the door, she glanced through the room. Decorated in soft hues, the space was cheerful. Now that her only child was nearing three years, she'd recently moved Sophie to a toddler's bed.

Jesse rested serenely in Sophie's old crib. Handcrafted, it was a beautiful piece, meant to be passed through many generations. A changing table and other baby items were nearby. Penelope shared Sophie's bed. The two girls slept soundly. A plethora of stuffed animals kept them safe from bad dreams.

Warmth gripped her inside as she gazed at the precious trio.

Doubt, so pressing when she'd woken, faded. Reason returned, giving her thoughts a not-so-gentle nudge.

When she and Josiah had wed, they'd hoped to begin having *kinder* right away. Alas, that had not happened. It had taken years for her to conceive. Her pregnancy had been a difficult one, and she was ordered to bed. Months later, she'd given birth to a healthy daughter. Embracing motherhood, she'd hoped for many more.

But it wasn't to be.

Nerves tightening, Lavinia reluctantly cast her thoughts back to the time after Josiah had passed. No one knew Sophie might have had a sibling. Barely eight weeks into her pregnancy, Lavinia had lost the *kind* she was carrying after his death. Unsure about her pregnancy, she hadn't had the chance to tell him he was going to be a *daed* again.

The secret was a heavy burden. Kneeling beside Josiah's grave on a cold winter's day, she'd asked him to look after their *kinder*. In her heart, she knew the little one would have been a *boi*, the son Josiah always wanted. Now they were together, safe in the Lord's loving embrace.

It had been a devastating blow. Had he lived and their *sohn* been born, perhaps Josiah would have seen the error of his ways and sought help for his addiction. They could have sold the house, moved to a smaller place and started over fresh.

Alas, it was not to be.

As the Bible said, the old passed away and the new must come.

Heart aching, Lavinia dropped her gaze. It wasn't hard to draw back the emotions she'd experienced after losing her *ehmann*. Shock. Anger. Confusion. She'd cycled through them all. Questioning. Searching. And, after a few months had passed, acceptance. Josiah's life had ended. Whatever the Lord had sent him to do had been done. As Josiah's body was returned to the ground, so had his soul been returned to his Creator.

Jesse snuffled in his sleep, letting out a soft sound. He began to fuss, flailing his arms and legs.

Concerned, Lavinia tiptoed into the room to check the *boppli*. With his blond hair and plump little cheeks, he was a handsome *boi*. Now six months, he was big enough to sleep in a crib. Having just gotten Sophie out of diapers, she'd forgotten how many times an infant needed to be fed and changed. It felt wonderful to have a *kleinkind* in her arms again—and exhausting!

Satisfied the *boppli* was dry and comfortable, she bent to retrieve a stuffed animal that had fallen off Sophie's bed. As she tucked it away, her gaze fell on little Penelope. Like Callie, she had a tangle of frizzy curls and a reddish complexion. Though they'd only met, the girls had become fast friends. A single child, Sophie was also a lonely one. Though she had cousins to play with, it wasn't the same as having a sibling.

Looking at the two, Lavinia cocked her head. Still a young and healthy woman, she wanted as many *kinder* as *Gott* would permit her to have.

The Lord always finds a way to answer our prayers. I see now why He sent Noem to my door. *Gott* had sent two *youngies* who needed a *mamm*. Penelope and Jesse were to be hers.

But that could only happen if she went through with the marriage.

Would it be so bad?

All the old feelings she'd once harbored for him rose to the surface, swirling through her memory. How would her life have gone if Noem had asked for her hand instead of Josiah? She knew he liked her. Callie had told her as much when they were teens. But he'd never said a word.

We were so young then.

By the time she'd entered her *rumspringa*, she and Josiah were walking out together. Most everyone in the Mueller and Simmons *families* approved of the pairing. Her *familie* liked and respected Josiah as a godly young man. They dated for almost two years. As her parents had passed years before, her eldest *bruder*, Rolf, had given his blessing for them to wed after Josiah had proposed. Having no real reason to say no, she'd accepted. When they'd turned eighteen, they'd wed.

Time and circumstance had parted her from

her friendships with Callie and Noem. But what if Callie hadn't been exaggerating about Noem's secret crush? In his time of need, he'd sought her out. Bishop Graber had, of course, given him a nudge. However, the bishop also knew of her dire dilemma. Working in the capacity of spiritual adviser and guidance counselor, the bishop had presented a solution that would help both out of a tight spot.

Dogged by uncertainty, Lavinia left the door half-open should Jesse cry or one of the girls awaken. Once Sophie woke, there would be no peace. Rested from a night's sleep, her *tochter* was a tiny terror, cycling through hours of tantrums, pouting and incessant queries.

Downstairs Lavinia crossed the living room and entered the kitchen. She filled the kettle with water and set it on the stove. Throughout the large living space, the furnishings were crafted in the sturdy style of early American. Crocheted afghans covered the sofa and sitting chairs. No photographs were present. But that didn't mean the house had a lot of blank walls. Elaborate needlework canvases were displayed, many quoting passages from the Bible. White lace curtains framed wide bay windows. Nothing was out of place, and everything served a purpose. The house was a cozy one.

But it wasn't hers anymore. Having closed on the deal, the new owners expected her to vacate.

Live with her relatives? Or marry Noem Witzel and have a home of her own?

She weighed the options. Except for Elam—who was single and a bachelor living an *Englisch* life—her other siblings had large *families* of their own. Why add to their burden? And how would she support herself? Like most Amish females, she'd been raised to believe a woman's place was in the home, rearing the *youngies*. Her limited education meant that the only thing she could do would be to clerk in the market Gran'pa Amos owned or wait tables at the local café. Having married at such a young age, she'd never held a job. The idea of going to work in the public frightened her. She'd always been a homebody.

The kettle whistled, breaking into her thoughts. After making a cup of stout black tea laced with sugar and cream, Lavinia sat down at the table. Early morning was her time to study her Bible and connect with the Lord. She relished her time alone with her Savior, spending time in prayer. In taking Josiah, the Lord had presented an alternative path for her to walk.

The heart plans our way, but Gott *establishes our steps.*

Her old life had ended. Now, like a butterfly emerging from a chrysalis, she must unfurl her wings and take flight toward an unknown destination. She knew she would stumble and fall. But above all those things, she knew she must stay focused on the Lord. As heartbreaking as it might be to the survivors left behind, she believed *Gott* had a way of organizing things in just the right way.

Rethinking her decision, she decided not to make the walk to the phone shanty. Practicality won over emotion.

It wasn't a love match. But it was a satisfactory solution to her predicament. And those who had lost a spouse were expected to remarry. The sooner, the better. *Familie* formation marriages were especially common when *kinder* were involved. Plain folks believed two parents were needed to rear *youngies* properly. No one would raise an eyebrow when Bishop Graber announced their impending nuptials after the Sunday service. Everyone would wish them well.

Staring into her empty cup, Lavinia forced herself to swallow back her doubt. The new road *Gott* presented had a fork. As the Lord had also given human beings free will, it was up to her to choose the direction she wished to take.

Her union with Noem Witzel would proceed.
A sigh pressed between her pursed lips.
Lord willing, we can make this work.

"Are you certain this is what you want to do,
sohn?" Gabriel Witzel asked. "You'll be mar-
ryin' a woman you barely know."

Clad in the suit he'd worn to Callie's burial,
Noem offered his parent a nod. "*Ja.* I think it's
best. Penelope and Jesse need a *mamm*. And
Lavinia will make a *gut* wife."

Gabriel reached out, straightening his shirt
collar. "But will she be a *gut* wife for you? She
might have been your friend once, but it's been
years since you two have socialized. You don't
know how she's changed."

"I know her better than you knew *mamm*,"
Noem countered. Having met as pen-pals, his
parents had courted by letter. "Didn't you meet
her only after you'd agreed to marry?" Born in
another state, his mother was Delaware Amish.

"Times were different then," Gabriel grumbled. "We wrote over two years."

"Lavinia and I went to school together for
eight years and then had *rumspringa*. We ran
in the same group then. I think that should
count for something. And I knew Josiah, too.
He was a *gut* fellow."

Gabriel's gaze darkened. Lines tightened

his brow. "Not as much as you might think. Word around is Josiah had some shady dealings with money. That's why Lavinia had to sell their place."

Noem frowned. He'd never had much use for gossip and rarely paid it any mind. "It's shameful for people to w-wag their tongues. Whatever Josiah did should have passed away with him."

"I wouldn't be so sure. Lavinia might yet have trouble you don't know about."

He refused to be deterred. "If she does, we'll cross that bridge when we come to it."

"Might be more than you can handle. A man who dies with secrets lies in an uneasy grave. *Gott* cautions us to keep our eyes open and not rush in like fools."

"*Gott* also cautions us not to rush to judgment." Refusing to let the ominous warning sway him, Noem set his hands on his *daed*'s shoulders. "Please, can't you be happy for me? I'll have an *ehefrau* and *youngies*. W-we can be a *familie* again. Like it was when Callie was living at home and *Mamm* was alive."

Stubbornness hardened Gabriel's jaw. "It won't be the same."

Noem sighed, letting his hands drop. "Nothing can ever be the same now that they are gone. But change is inevitable. *Gott* says our days will fade as the season changes. As painful as it is, why can't we find joy when new people come into our lives? *Gott* sent us Callie's *kinder*. He wanted them here, with us."

"The right thing would be to give them to their *dat*'s *familie*. Let them grow up in the *Englisch* world."

Forcing himself to hold his tongue, Noem tamped down his anger and disappointment. "We've had this argument. I've made up my m-mind."

Truth be told, he'd never intended to marry and have *youngies*. He didn't have anything against the idea of the institution. His biggest problem—if it could even be called a problem—was that he liked his own company better than he liked people. He was content to tinker with his projects. Part of that, he supposed, was because of the stutter he'd suffered since early childhood. His tongue tripped over the simplest words, making him feel like a blundering fool. The kids at school teased him mercilessly, leading him to withdraw from playgroups. Alone, he didn't have to talk. He could read, think and work with his hands. But the more time he spent on his own, the less he wanted to socialize.

Come *rumspringa*, he'd dated a few girls, going on a walkabout or two. But nothing serious panned out. Didn't matter. He liked being a bachelor. He answered to no one and did as he wanted. Working in Zeb Yoder's buggy shop, he customized the vehicles with modern equipment that would make the quaint conveyances safer on public roads. With the addition of brake lights and other features, Amish buggies were quite sophisticated.

Having worked for Zeb since the age of sixteen, he'd recently learned his boss planned to sell the shop and retire. Having accumulated a tidy bit of money, Noem intended to approach the old man about buying the business. He planned to make an offer when the time was right. A couple of other fellows he worked with also intended to put in their bids. He wanted to be the first in line, with cash in hand.

It would be a trade I could pass to Jesse.

Thoughts tumbled through his mind. It was frightening and exciting to know he was going to be a *familie* man. In less than a week, he'd gone from footloose and fancy-free to nervously waiting to marry a woman he'd never even asked on a date.

"If you're gettin' cold feet, now is the time to say so," Gabriel warned. "No one would blame you if you backed out."

The idea enticed. Noem refused to let it take

root. Doubt was an insidious potion, threading a man's thoughts like clinging vines.

"I can't do that. Lavinia's sold her house, and the new owners want her out."

"She has a large *familie*. And the Muellers are well off. They could easily make a place for her."

"I don't think that's what she wants. Once a woman has had her own home, she's used to doing things her way."

Gabriel crossed his arms. "And I suppose she'll be wantin' to change things around when she's under *my* roof," he said, releasing a huff.

Noem resisted rolling his eyes. It was one thing to be a single man and live with his *daed*. But it was quite another trying to move an *ehe-frau* and *kinder* in.

"We won't be staying forever. I'm planning to buy a piece of property and build a proper home. One with plenty of rooms for all the *youngies*." As it was, the simple one-story house he'd grown up in was small. Without a doubt, elbows were sure to get jostled, and nerves would be strained.

"Going to be a tight fit for six," his *daed* warned.

"We could always fix up the *dawdy haus*. It's been empty since *Oma* passed."

Gabriel gave him a deep frown. "*Ach*, tryin' to throw me out of my own house already."

"I'm trying to think of a way to make this w-work."

Nostrils flaring, Gabriel doubled down. "I believe it won't. But since you refuse to hear me out, I've no more to say." Shoulders stiffening, he marched out of the room. Entrenched in anger, the old man seemed determined to complain until the very last minute.

Left alone, Noem took a minute to reflect.

After Lavinia had agreed to become his *ehefrau*, the matter of when and where to hold the nuptials had arisen. Normally, a wedding was an event that would see friends and *familie* joining the celebration. The couple usually didn't announce their engagement until a few weeks before their joining was to take place. At that time, preparations would begin.

As a widow, Lavinia wouldn't be entitled to a second elaborate celebration. Out of respect for her deceased spouse, she'd be expected to remarry quietly and without fanfare. Bishop Graber had decided they would tie the knot later in the afternoon, after Sunday services. As Noem and Lavinia attended church in different districts, Bishop Graber's wife had offered to host the ceremony at their home. Only immediate *familie* would attend. As head of the church, the bishop would officiate.

Marrying Lavinia meant he got a *tagesmutter* for his niece and nephew. In exchange, she got a home and the respectability of a married woman. It was more of a business proposition than a love match.

But was it the right thing to do? When the Amish wed, it was for life. Divorce could never be an option. Once joined, their coupling would be expected to last unto death. Amish men and women were expected to stay together and tough out the bad times. That's the way it was. That's the way it always would be.

"In for a penny, in for a pound," he muttered.

A knock at the door interrupted.

"Come in."

The door cracked open. Letty Graber, the bishop's wife, peeped in. "We are ready."

He smoothed a few wrinkles out of his vest. "Just one more minute."

"Of course," Letty said and withdrew.

Gazing in a decorative mirror hung on the wall, Noem gave himself a last nervous check. His attempt to tame his curls was unsuccessful. No matter how hard he tried, his hair would always be an unruly mess. His bangs curtained his forehead, brushing his eyes. He ran his hands over his bare cheeks. Freshly shaved, not a sign of stubble remained. In the Amish community, an unmarried man couldn't grow his beard out until after he wed. Bound in holy matrimony, he'd be obligated to grow out his facial hair. Though he didn't care for the look, the *Ordnung* allowed a man to wear his hair in a style trimmed to a reasonable length.

No backing out now.

Exiting the small antechamber where he'd been told to wait, Noem walked into the adjoining space. The bishop's den was sparse, holding only a desk and a few chairs to accommodate visitors. It was a space befitting a man who served the church and his community with humility and wisdom.

As expected, most of the Mueller *familie* had turned out to see Lavinia remarried. Her *groossdaadi* had also consented to attend. Aside from looking a little cranky, Amos Mueller said nothing much.

As Lavinia couldn't get married with a handful of *kinder*, her *schwester*, Annalise, kept Sophie and Penelope quiet. Touchingly, she had taken the time to fix Penelope's hair, adding colorful ribbons to her neat braids. Her sister-in-law Frannie held Jesse.

Noem looked to the Witzel side. Sadly, only his *daed* was present. Aside from Penelope and Jesse, he had no other relatives living in Wisconsin.

No one said a word. The mood of the room was muted and respectful. If nothing else, the Amish were levelheaded people. Death happened. Life went on. Those left behind picked up the pieces and continued the pilgrimage.

Forcing himself to calm down, Noem stepped into the groom's place. His gaze found and rested on Lavinia. Save for her white apron and *kapp*, she still dressed as a widow in mourning. Though she'd done up her hair in a tight bun, she hadn't tamed her thick mane. A few wisps curled around her nape. Other stray wisps brushed her pale cheeks.

Pride wound its way through his insides. "You look beautiful," he murmured.

Gaze lifting, Lavinia offered him a nod. Abram's wife, Maddie, stood as her attendant. Noem's *daed* stood on the groom's side. The set of Gabriel's jaw and stiffness in his posture revealed his disapproval.

Knowing he didn't have his *daed*'s blessing, Noem felt his stomach twist into knots. Heart beating double time, he wished he'd taken the time to pray. Though he was baptized and attended church, he rarely visited with the Lord. Once Sunday services ended, he tucked away his Bible and didn't give it a second look. Having lost touch with his faith, he'd found he didn't miss it. Until today.

Please, Gott, *don't let this be one giant mistake.*

James Graber eyed the group. "Before we proceed, I must ask if anyone has an objection to this union."

Tongue scraping dry lips, Noem tensed. The wait for someone to break the silence was excruciating.

Thankfully, no one on the Mueller side voiced any concerns.

Neither did Gabriel.

"Then we shall proceed." Instructing them to join hands, Bishop Graber began the ceremony.

Straightening his shoulders, Noem prepared himself to recite the vows that would bind him to Lavinia Simmons through the entirety of his life.

In the back of his mind, he knew it was a sham. She'd admitted she could never love him. And that was fine. He wasn't marrying for affection or even companionship. Their union was a convenience.

He expected nothing more.

The wipers beat back and forth in a steady rhythm across the windshield. Though turned on high, they barely cut through the sheets of water pouring down from the sky. A fierce wind buffeted the vehicle, causing it to swerve into the oncoming lane.

"This weather is something else." The *Englisch* driver threw the words over his shoulder. Hands welded to the wheel, he stared straight ahead, fighting to navigate through the drenching rain without wrecking the van.

Stomach in knots, Lavinia peered through the window. "I think we should pull over," she said, glancing at the *youngies* strapped into the car seats. Another storm had blown in during the afternoon, sending down a torrent of rain. Bishop Graber had loaned them the use of the church van and driver to deliver them to the Witzel home. Taking a buggy in such dangerous weather wouldn't only be impractical, it would be downright dangerous.

Exhausted by their long day, the three *youngies* slept as only little ones could. Still sulking over the entire situation, Gabriel sat enveloped in sullen silence.

The wedding party wasn't a happy one. Everyone was stressed. The addition of the thunderstorm stretched nerves even tighter.

Refusing to view the downpour as a warning of things to come in her marriage, Lavinia declined to let ominous thoughts take root. Instead, she focused on hope and faith and the *gut* things to come tomorrow.

Sitting beside her, Noem reached for her hand. "It's just another few miles. We'll make it."

Uneasy, she tightened her grip on the door and held on for dear life. "From your mouth to *Gott*'s ears." The chance of hitting a slick spot that might send them spinning out of control increased with every passing second. The Witzels lived down a long stretch of rural road outside Humble. Surrounded by a patch of densely wooded land, it was a place you had to go looking for to locate.

Turning down a gravel road, the driver followed twisting curves through the property. Minutes later, he rolled to a stop. "We made it."

Lavinia silently thanked the Lord. The storm, however, wasn't ready to end. The rain tripled its fury. Lightning forked the sky, blinding in its intensity. A rolling crash of thunder rattled the earth.

Noem squeezed her hand. "Welcome to your new home."

Reassured by his touch, she felt a hitch stall her breath. *"Danke."*

Leaning forward, she gazed out the window. In her youth, she'd visited the Witzel property many times. Back then, the white-

washed house sat snug inside a fenced-in yard.
A ring of sturdy walnut trees provided shade
in the summer and a windbreak from winter weather. The lawn and gardens had been
well-kept. Amelia Witzel, Noem's *mamm*, had
taken pride in her petunias, planting a variety
of bright colors.

But nothing such as that greeted her eyes.
The property had fallen to ruin. The wooden
fence had gone down in places, leaving great
gaps that resembled a mouth full of broken
teeth. The gardens were in absolute disarray.
The petunias had withered away, and the once-
lovely bluegrass was tangled and unkempt.
Thankfully, the house seemed to have fared
a little better. The screened-in porch sagged,
but at least it looked solid enough to walk on.

Catching her expression, Noem offered a
weak smile. "I know it's not much, but I'll get
us something better. Soon. I promise."

"Don't know why this house isn't *gut*
enough," Gabriel grumbled.

Lavinia managed a stiff nod. When Amelia was alive, she'd taken immaculate care of
her home and gardens. After she had passed,
years of neglect and weather had taken a toll.

"It's fine," she said, forcing herself to speak.
"I'm thankful for a roof over my head."

Noem chanced a smile. "At least the roof doesn't leak. You'll be dry—if nothing else."

Forcing a smile and a nod, Lavinia swallowed back the expectation she'd had. *Gott* had certainly presented a challenge she hadn't been prepared for. She went from having a comfortable, decent home to a sad eyesore in need of a loving hand to restore it. It was quite a comedown. Confidence wavering, her pride took a hard blow.

But there was no turning back. She couldn't unmarry Noem. If she sought a divorce, she'd be excommunicated. Shunned.

The idea was unthinkable. Unacceptable on every level.

Whether she liked it or not, she was now Mrs. Noem Witzel. And that meant she was stuck for the long haul. It was too late to change her mind or walk away.

Pressing a hand against the window, she leaned her forehead against the rain-flecked glass and closed her eyes.

Please, Lord, help me turn this hovel into a home.

Chapter Four

Hoping the inside of the house would be more welcoming, Lavinia unlatched her seat belt. Gas-powered vehicles had never been a favored way of traveling, but she tolerated their use when necessary. Her preference would always be a buggy.

The rain continued to pour, turning the ground into a mess. The only way to get through it was to make a quick dash to the porch.

"I'll get Jesse and you grab the girls," she said, reaching for the infant's travel bag. "They'll just have to get wet."

"I could do without this rain," Noem said, helping unstrap the little ones.

Gabriel stepped into the rain. "*Kinder* aren't made from sugar," he grumbled. "They won't melt."

"I'd prefer not to have three runny noses,"

she countered, wrapping baby Jesse in a blanket to shield him from the damp. Unhappy with the jostling, the *boppli* burst into cries of distress.

Unbuckling Sophie and Penelope, Noem then bundled them into a bear hug. Their arms circled his neck. Holding them close, he dashed toward the screened-in porch. Sullen-faced, Gabriel followed. Lavinia trailed the two men, thankful to leave the rain behind. The yard might be in disarray, but at least the promise of a solid roof was sincere.

After seeing them safely inside, the *Englisch* driver disappeared down the drive.

Holding Jesse close, Lavinia glanced over the property. A lot of water had gone under the bridge since she'd last visited the Witzel home. Back when she and Callie were teens, the porch was a comfortable spot to hang out on a sweltering summer day. They'd often sit on the bench swing, sipping lemonade and working on their needlepoint. Noem was usually nearby, spending an hour or so turning the crank on an old wooden churn to make a batch of homemade ice cream. Amelia Witzel supervised, snapping peas for the evening meal. Always a woman with a green thumb, her pride was her flower boxes. Filled with a variety of blooms, the plants lent a quaint charm to the space.

The swing was still in place, swaying gently. But the flower boxes, like the gardens, were allowed to wither.

Opening the front door, Gabriel let everyone inside.

Steeling her nerve, Lavinia followed him. Most everything was as she remembered, but a lot worse for wear. It looked like ages had passed since anyone had dusted or swept the floors. The curtains were frayed. Cobwebs haunted high corners.

Schooling her face to a neutral expression, Lavinia tamped down her inner conflict. Though filled with memories, the house lacked joy. There was no warmth, only a deteriorating and ignored shell.

Noticing her noticing the mess, Noem winced. "Going to take a bit of elbow grease to clean it up. We hired an *Englisch* housekeeper. But she said it was too much work and quit."

"Men have elbows, too," she countered, lifting Jesse to her shoulder to calm him with a pat on the back. The infant's cries turned to a sniffle of discontent. Having had a long afternoon, he was tired and fussy. Penelope and Sophie were also out of their element. Confused by the unfamiliar place, Sophie clung to Lavinia's skirt. The comfortable house she'd known all her life was gone, throwing the toddler into turmoil. Having only spent a brief time in the care of her *onkel* and *grobvater*, Penelope, too, was disoriented. Abandoned by her *daed*, she'd also lost her *mamm* in a sudden and upsetting way. She still hadn't grasped the finality of death and had asked after Callie time and time again.

"The house is fine," Gabriel said through a huff. "Does what we need it to do."

Noem shot his parent a frown. "I know you're not happy with the changes in our living space, but it's temporary. We will get a place of our own."

"And then you'll move out and leave me all alone," the old man returned, spoiling for an argument.

Noem sighed with frustration. "It's not th-that way at all. Of course, we would love to s-stay. But if you're going to sulk, there's no reason. Lavinia is my wife. I won't have you being disrespectful to her."

"Why don't you just take over everything?" Unhappy, Gabriel walked to the back door to retrieve the rain slicker hanging nearby. "Need to feed the horses," he mumbled before departing.

Lavinia watched him go. Her new *schwiegervater* was proving to be a hard pill to swallow. She'd also noticed Noem's childhood stutter had returned. Back when they were in school, the impediment had dogged him without mercy. He was as nervous and as uncomfortable as she was.

As if embarrassed, Noem gave her a look. "I apologize. I'd hoped he'd be more welcoming."

"He doesn't seem happy," she commented tactfully, doing her best to soothe the wailing infant.

"I'm ashamed of his sulking. I'm going to put my foot down and demand that you be treated with respect."

Doubtful, Lavinia kept her thoughts to herself. Looking around, she couldn't imagine ever being happy in the dreary old house. Passing under the threshold was like taking a step back in time, at least a century or more. Instead of the modern appliances she was used to, those populating the kitchen were sadly out of date. Cooking would have to be done on a monstrous wood-burning stove. Cast in black iron, the massive old thing was at least a century in age. The icebox, too, was an antique— one well recognized in the area and built in the state of Wisconsin in the eighteenth century. To cool perishables, blocks of ice were cut from the ponds in the winter and kept for use throughout the year. Going back generations, many Amish still used their cellars for the storage of preserved meats, vegetables and other edibles.

"I promise we won't be here forever," Noem said. "As it is, six of us will almost be nose to nose."

And there lay the crux of the matter. Most Amish homes were spacious and rambling, with plenty of room for a large and growing *familie*. The Witzels' house was only a single story and compact. The kitchen and living room flowed together, which better allowed the stove and fireplace to heat the home in winter. There were three bedrooms: a master and two smaller ones. The largest bedroom had an attached bath. A second washroom was between the two single bedrooms. Callie had often complained about having to share with her brother, stating that he hogged the tub more than she did.

Jesse set to fussing again, prompting Lavinia to check his diaper. "He needs a change."

Noem motioned for her to follow. "You and the *youngies* will have the back bedrooms. You'll have Callie's old room, and the *kinder* can have my room."

Her brows rose. "If the *youngies* have your room and I have Callie's, where will you stay?"

"I'm bunking with *Daed*. All I need is a cot in the corner, so it's not putting him out," he explained, opening the door to his former quarters.

Passing the threshold, Lavinia blinked. A stack of boxes sat near a full-size bed and night table. Save for a fitted sheet, the bed was stripped bare. Covered in an unappealing shade of beige, the walls were dull.

She gave him a puzzled look. "I thought you went to Wausau to pick up their things."

Noem spread his hands toward the boxes. "There wasn't much to get. Callie and the *kinder* were living in a motel. It looks like she lost almost everything after Erik left. Aside from some clothes and toys, they had nothing else. When I talked to the manager, he told me Callie was behind on the rent and about to be evicted when she got sick."

"How terrible!"

"I did not know how dreadful things were." Upset, he rubbed his face. The dark circles under his eyes showed he'd not had a good night's rest in days. "I meant to have the place ready for you and the *youngies*, but nothing worked out." His lips flattened into a tight line.

Penelope looked around and caught sight of her toys sticking out of a box. "Is Mamma coming?"

Lavinia cast a glance toward Noem. "We should tell her." Through the days she'd kept the *youngies*, Penelope kept asking for her *mamm*. Unsure whether it was her place to tell the little girl about Callie's passing, she'd said nothing.

A panicked expression creased Noem's face. "What do I say?"

Having been through the dilemma herself, Lavinia knew firsthand how difficult it was to speak about the end of life to a *youngie*. As her *tochter* was too young to understand Josiah's passing, she'd never had to sit down and explain to Sophie why her *daadi* wasn't in their lives anymore. But at well past four years, Penelope would have a better comprehension of loss, even though she might not fully grasp the true meaning of death.

"Shall I tell her?"

"Bitte." Noem's throat visibly tightened with emotion. "I can't. I—I just can't."

Penelope tugged at her skirt. "Can I see Mamma?"

Holding the sopping *boppli*, Lavinia glanced down. Not the best time, but the matter needed to be addressed. Laying Jesse on the bed, she sat down on the edge. Extending her arms, she reached for Penelope and drew her close.

"Your *mamm* can't come home because she has died," she said, using simple words.

Eyes tearing up, the little girl's face crumbled. "Why?"

"When someone dies, their body stops working. When that happens, they go away to heaven."

Penelope's lower lip began to tremble. "But Mamma went to see the doctor-man. Can't he make her better?"

Lavinia slowly shook her head. "Sometimes there isn't anything the doctor can do. But you mustn't be sad. Your *mamm* is with *Gott* now. He will take *gut* care of her."

Penelope's small body shook. "But I want Mamma," she said, releasing a piteous cry.

Emotions ripping over the *youngie*'s grief, Lavinia hugged her tighter. "There, there, little one," she crooned. "Everything will be all right."

Affected by her friend's tears, Sophie ran up and offered a hug out of sympathy. "I share Mamma," she whispered, petting Penelope's hair with a gentle hand.

Noem stepped up, swooping his niece into his strong embrace. "It's okay to cry," he said, settling her against his shoulder. "We will take *gut* care of you."

Penelope circled his neck with her small arms and laid her head on his shoulder. "I want my mamma."

Sensing the *kind* needed comfort, Noem rocked her. He hummed a familiar Amish lullaby, singing in a soft voice. After a few minutes, Penelope's body relaxed. Exhausted, the child slipped into the merciful hands of sleep.

"Rest, little one," he murmured. "May *Gott* watch over you and bring only happy dreams."

Lavinia looked at him with admiration. Instead of backing away from the child's grief, he'd embraced it. "That's what Penelope needs. A lot of love and care from her *familie*."

Hugging his niece close, he nodded. "I know it will take time and patience for the *kinder* to heal."

An immense and completely unfamiliar tenderness filled her. The regret and disappointment she'd experienced earlier began to fade. "*Gott* willing, we will be a *familie*."

"*Gott* willing," he returned, smiling.

Needing to tend to the squirming *boppli*, Lavinia gave her attention to Jesse. "Let me get him changed. Then I'll make up the bed for the girls to sleep in." She glanced around the otherwise bare room. "It'll have to do until we can get the furniture moved in."

"I'll buy some of the things they need tomorrow."

Lavinia shook her head. "You don't have to." Digging in the travel bag for a fresh diaper and wet wipes, she glanced over her shoulder. "I was wondering what to do with Sophie's crib and changing table. And she and Penelope have been sharing a bed, so that will work awhile longer. We can certainly fit in the dresser and armoire, too."

"You're not upset?"

"Why would I be? Getting angry won't solve the problem."

Noem placed a protective hand across Penelope's back. "It's all so m-much."

"You're making a mountain out of a molehill," she said, drawing on the deep well of calm a woman needed to deal with life's trials. "The rain will stop, and we can start moving our things. While the rooms are empty, we can freshen things up. A coat of paint will do wonders."

The lines creasing his brow smoothed. "When you say it that way, it doesn't sound so bad."

"I'd rather find a solution than cry over the problem."

Spurred by enthusiasm, he scanned the walls. "I'll go to the hardware store and buy the paint tomorrow. What colors would you like?"

Encouraged, she mulled the options. He seemed willing to follow her suggestions.

"White would look nice, with a color for

the trim. Perhaps a pale yellow to brighten the room."

"Yellow sounds nice," he agreed amiably.

Glancing around, she nodded approval. "A little paint, sweeping the floor... This will make a fine nursery for the *youngies*." The bare space was uninviting, but that didn't mean it had to stay that way.

"I like the way you look at things." A smile lightened his striking features. "It's about time this old house had some life back in it. It's been filled with sadness too long."

Lavinia pursed her lips. For all the plusses she'd uncovered, there was still one negative to be conquered. "I know Gabriel isn't happy, but we will try to stay out of his way."

Noem's gaze locked on hers. "As long as you are here, this is your home. I know the place is small, but it's only temporary. I promise."

Finished with her task, she tickled Jesse. His stubby legs kicked the air. Picking him up, she balanced the *boppli* on her hip with a practiced move. Comfortable in her care, the little *boi* gurgled with contentment.

"I have no complaints. I'm grateful we'll have a place to lay our heads."

It wasn't the way she'd envisioned spending her first night in her new home. Still, she trusted Bishop Graber was right when he'd recommended the union. She and Noem shared a common background, and each had a need the other could fill. The Lord taught that a man and a woman were to bear one another's burdens.

She'd taken a vow to be her *ehmann*'s helpmate.

She intended to honor it.

The house might not be in the best shape, but she could work with what she had at hand. If it meant rolling up her sleeves and tearing in all by herself, then so be it.

Leaving Lavinia to unpack a few things, Noem headed toward the barn. Puffed up like a brooding pigeon, Gabriel hadn't said a civil word to her. If they were going to be living under the same roof, it would be better for all concerned if everyone could live together peacefully. Given how much had happened since he'd taken custody of Penelope and Jesse, Noem believed he'd handled things logically. Now that he'd taken an *ehefrau*, finding a home for their extended *familie* would have to be his priority. It was a biblically sound principle, and one he intended to follow. He could only hope his *daed* would want to be a part of their lives.

Having exited through the back door, Noem dashed through the rain. The downpour had lessened, settling into a gentle patter. A flash of lightning warned the storm wasn't done, though. The barn loomed ahead, offering shelter to the animals kept on the property. Living on the outskirts of Humble allowed them to keep a large variety of livestock. Aside from horses, there were a few cows and goats.

As he walked inside, the scent of hay tickled his nostrils. Neat and well-kept, the barn was lit by battery-powered lamps. Gabriel worked in a nearby stall, cleaning out the old bedding and adding in fresh hay. A farrier by trade, his father loved all things horses. He spent hours with his equines, currying them until their coats shined. Their feed was a custom mix, and they often received an apple or carrots as a treat.

Noem slipped out of his wet slicker and hung it on a peg. He was expected to follow in the same trade when he'd left school at fourteen. But he'd tried the work for a couple of years and found he didn't like it. Creating horseshoes from red-hot iron took a lot of skill, as did the ability to clean, trim and shape a horse's hooves. It was also dangerous work. An out-of-control horse could cause injury or death. Gabriel had done the work for nigh on forty years, as had his *daed* and his *groossdaadi* before him.

Noem grabbed a pitchfork. "Need a hand?"

Gabriel glanced up. "*Nein*. Almost finished."

Ignoring him, Noem forked up fresh hay. "I hope you're hungry. Lavinia said she'd have supper on the table in an hour."

The older man frowned. "Guess she's going to be takin' over your *mamm*'s kitchen."

"*Ja*. She is. Things are going to be a little different from now on, but that doesn't mean you have to get bent out of shape."

Gabriel didn't look up. "I like things the way they are."

Halting his work, Noem leaned against his pitchfork. If they started arguing, it would all fall apart. Staying in control of the situation was strictly up to him.

It's time for healing to begin.

Gathering his patience, he said, "No. I don't think you do. Since Callie went away and *Mamm* passed, you've been living like the walking dead. You don't care about anyone or anything but your horses. I know you're hurt. But lashing out just to make others feel awful isn't the way to treat people who have done nothing to you. Lavinia's a kind woman. If you give her a chance, she will be a *gut schwiegertochter*."

"Never said she wouldn't be." Pausing, Gabriel propped his pitchfork against the wall before digging in a pocket to retrieve a handkerchief. "I remember when she'd visit Callie," he said, giving his rheumy eyes and nose a wipe. "Always did like her."

"I did, too. When she started seeing Josiah, I'd hoped it wouldn't work out. I always wanted to ask her to take a walkabout, but it never happened."

Snuffling, Gabriel tucked his handkerchief away. "If you had a yen for her, you should have elbowed Josiah aside. That's what I did with your *mamm*."

Noem's brows rose. That was news.

"Really?"

Gabriel nodded. "Amelia was writin' two of us fellas, tryin' to make up her mind which she wanted to marry. It's hard when you're doin' your courtin' by mail, but that's the way it was back then. I knew by her letters the other fella was gettin' the edge on me."

"What did you do?"

"I hired a driver and made the trip to Delaware." Seemingly caught up in the memory, the old man chuckled. "Had my best suit and some pretty flowers for her. Gardenias, as I recall. Those were her favorite." Unexpectedly tickled, he slapped one knee. "I was nervous when I knocked on her door. She answered, and I proposed."

"You never told me that story before."

Face going ruddy, Gabriel coughed behind his hand. "Some things, um, they're special between a man and his sweetheart. It was our secret, just for us. Won't say we didn't have our ups and downs. But we had over thirty years together. I know I don't say it, but I praise *Gott* for sendin' me Amelia. When the Lord took her home…" Overcome with memories, he drifted into silence.

"I know you miss *Mamm* every day."

"She was my whole life." The old man's hands trembled, as did his voice. "When she passed, it felt like I did, too."

Noem understood then why his *daed* had grown distant and disinterested. Years ago, when their *familie* was whole, everyone would gather around the table in the morning for Bible study and prayer. And then everything changed, throwing their lives into chaos. Callie went under the *bann*. His *mamm* took to her bed. Refusing to see a doctor, Amelia never stood on her own two feet again. And, come *rumspringa*, he had his own life to pursue. Eager to get out the door in the morning, he'd also stopped coming to the table.

That left Gabriel sitting. Waiting. Alone.

He'd believed it was his *daed* who'd changed. He was wrong. He was the one who'd changed.

Gabriel wasn't distant because he didn't care. He was distant because he did. His losses had psychologically scarred him. Keeping his distance was his way of shielding himself from more emotional trauma.

I never saw things from his side.

Shame filled him. He should have known better as a churchgoing man, but he was tied up in his own concerns. *Gott* warned foolish children were a sorrow to their parents. Sadness and despair had taken a heavy toll on Gabriel. It would take time, but perhaps he could help undo some of the damage.

Noem set his hand on his *daed*'s shoulder. "I know we haven't been close in the last few years, but I'd like that to change. I've got an *ehefrau* and *youngies* to raise. I'd be willing to listen to the advice of a man who has been there."

Wiping his eyes again, Gabriel then blew his nose before tucking away his handkerchief. "Can't say I have the answers for you," he admitted after clearing his throat. "I didn't do such a *gut* job with your *schwester*."

Letting his hand drop, Noem shook his head. "Callie made her choices. *Gott* gives us free will, and she chose to go *Englisch*. I know it pains you she broke her vow to the church, but we must let her rest in peace now that she's gone. The Lord will have His reckoning with her in His own *gut* time."

"That's true. We all come to our judgment."

"We can remember the *gut* things about Callie and pray *Gott* has mercy on her. I would want the same for myself."

"You've never given a day's trouble to anyone," Gabriel said, offering an unexpected compliment. "You've grown into a responsible man. Your *mamm* would be pleased you're tryin' to do the right thing for Callie's *kinder*. I know if she'd lived, she would have taken the *youngies* herself."

"Then you're not mad?"

Resignation sifted past the old man's lips. "I guess I'm angrier Callie didn't think we would care. I know she was shunned, but the *Ordnung* gives us allowances that would've let us have a visit with her and the *youngies*—to see after their needs. To my dyin' day, I'll regret not seein' her before she left this earth. May the Lord forgive me for bein' so harsh. Now she's gone, and it's too late to make amends."

Brushing aside a few wisps of stray hair, Noem let out a breath. "We can't undo the mistakes we all made."

"That *Englischer* Callie married—I never trusted him to do right by her. I warned her, but she wouldn't listen," Gabriel murmured sadly. "Broke Amelia's heart she chose such a man. *Gott* rest your *mamm*'s soul. I wish I was with her."

"But you're still here," Noem said softly. "And Penelope and Jesse will need their *groossdaadi* to help see them grow."

"Been a long time since we had *youngies* here." The older man snuffled with amusement. "Got set in my ways."

Relieved to have found common ground, Noem laughed. "Oh, three active *youngies* under five are sure to unset those ways soon, I'm sure."

"Suppose they will." A question wreathed the older man's expression. "What about Lavinia? Have you talked about havin' more?"

"We agreed to three," Noem said, answering with truth. "There probably won't be *kinder* of our own. We both know we didn't marry for love."

"You can't be sure." Gabriel cocked his head. "Why, Lavinia's *daed* and *mamm* were matched, too."

"Is that so?"

"It's true. Nathan Mueller's first *ehefrau* passed young, leavin' him with Rolf and Abram to raise. A few months later, Bishop Strohl introduced him to the Widow Jaeger. She had no *kinder*, but she was willin' to take on those two *bois* of his. Anyway, the Lord blessed them and they had four more, includin' Lavinia. They were together until the day they died."

Noem dug back in his memory. Lavinia was just a teenager when her *daed* and *mamm* were in a buggy accident. An *Englisch* driver was at fault. No one survived.

"Do you think there's a chance we could have a proper marriage?"

"Feelin's can grow between two people who respect one another."

Doubt thumped Noem. "I don't know if that's possible. She's still grieving for Josiah. As for changing our agreement—" A shrug rolled off his shoulders.

"Have you thought about courtin' her?"

Noem returned a quizzical gaze. "But we're already married. That's the point of dating, right? To get a *fraulein* to marry you."

Hand slapping his forehead, Gabriel rolled his eyes. "*Ach*, no wonder you hadn't a chance of findin' a bride without draggin' two *kinder* behind you. There's not a romantic bone in your body."

"Speaking of r-romance…" he countered, inwardly wincing over the delicate subject. "I never even saw you give *Mamm* a kiss on the cheek."

Gabriel nailed him with a frown. "Kissin' is for private. And if you want kisses, you'll have to earn them."

"How?"

"Do for Lavinia the way I did for your *mamm*." Reclaiming his pitchfork, Gabriel set to finishing the stall. "You think I enjoyed sittin' in the buggy while Amelia gabbed with her friends or shopped at the market? Or buildin' those flower boxes?" Forking up more hay, he shook his head. "Nope. Not one bit. But I did it because it made her happy. And she did the same for me. Mendin' my clothes and puttin' a meal on the table. That's what we did. Took care of each other."

His *daed*'s words resonated in a way Noem hadn't expected. The pieces of the puzzle fell into place, revealing the bigger picture. His parents had lived a biblically sound life, abiding by the principles of marriage as set down by the Lord. Fulfilling their roles as man and wife, they gave to each other in so many ways. Thoughtful acts of kindness revealed the depth of their affection.

"You mean I need to woo Lavinia?"

Standing straight, Gabriel nodded emphatically. "That's exactly what I'm sayin'."

Chapter Five

Pleased with his handiwork, Noem stepped away from the wall. After a long morning's work, he'd finished painting the bedrooms.

"What do you think?"

Boppli propped on her hip, Lavinia peeked inside. Her gaze swept the room from top to bottom. "*Ach*, it's beautiful."

"I'm glad you like it." For a clean, modern look, he'd chosen an off-white. It had taken two coats to cover the dingy old wallpaper on the walls, but the extra effort had paid off. The new color had opened the space. He'd also done the trim in sunshine yellow. The space would be comfortable once the furniture was in place.

A smile tugged at the corners of her lips. Squeezing Jesse, she snuggled him close. "Don't you have such a pretty room now?"

"Gaa!" Arms flailing, the *boppli* set to squealing with delight. "Ahm, goo!"

Noem laughed. "I hope I've got his stamp of approval."

Thoughts rolling back to the previous day, he recalled the look on Lavinia's face when they'd first arrived. Though she hadn't said an unkind word, dismay haunted her gaze. Knowing the house from past times, she'd most likely expected better. Half-ashamed of what he had to offer, he'd decided to make the repairs. He'd promised a decent home for her and Sophie. Not a dump she'd be embarrassed by. He intended to keep his word.

Up before dawn, he'd waited until eight a.m.—when the hardware store would be open—before heading into town with a long list. Paint, brushes, duct tape and a multitude of other items had filled his basket. He'd also ordered the lumber and nails needed for repairs on the veranda and fence. As he couldn't load those onto a buggy, he'd arranged to have them delivered later in the day. His *daed* did not know what he had planned, but he hoped Gabriel would approve.

"It looks entirely different. I'm amazed at what a little paint can do to spruce things up," Lavinia said.

"Would you like to see your room?"

"Can I?"

"You can." Laying the roller on a piece of foil,

Noem swiped the back of his arm across his perspiring brow. Even with the windows thrown open to let in the breeze, he'd still worked up a sweat. A dull ache pressed behind his eyes, but he didn't pay it much mind.

Leading the way, he crossed to Callie's old room. Having asked Lavinia not to look until he'd finished, he opened the door. Covering her walls in the same shade of white, he'd done the accents in a pale lilac shade. He'd also thrown the shutters wide, allowing a burst of bright sunlight to stream in. With the window open, a spring breeze filled the entire space with fresh air. Thankfully, the night's rain had passed. The sky above was clear, with nary a cloud in sight.

"What do you think?"

Mouth dropping open, Lavinia walked in. "It's beautiful." Moisture rimmed her lashes. "I didn't expect you would get it done so fast."

Warmed by her response, Noem felt a twisty sensation curl its way around his heart. Doing a job well had always given him a sense of satisfaction. But it was an entirely different feeling to do something special for the woman he now called his *ehefrau*. The Bible taught that a man was to take care of his helpmate. Once, he'd believed that to mean providing the necessities. Now he realized it meant so much more. The advice his *daed* had offered took on a greater meaning. Love wasn't grand gestures. Love was kindness, doing jobs that would help a woman turn a house into a home.

"I'm doing the bathroom, too. And then I'm taking you to pick out new washcloths, towels and rugs. You know, to spruce it up."

"Are you sure you want to spend the money? I have things from the old house I can use."

"You deserve to have a few new things."

Lavinia glanced around. "You really shouldn't spend more money when I can repurpose or remake a lot of things." She paused, and then added, "If that's okay."

"Whatever you want to do is fine." Noem shook his head. "I can't remember the last time those old curtains were taken down and washed. I'm sure they need to be tossed. The rugs, too, need to be replaced."

Hitching baby Jesse onto her hip, she laughed. "*Ach*, men left on their own are a disaster." She left the bedroom and crossed through the living room and into the kitchen.

Noem trailed in her wake. A slew of girlish giggles filled the living room.

"I wondered where they'd gone."

Both Penelope and Sophie had been under his feet until Lavinia took both in hand, shooing them away so he could work in peace. To keep the girls busy, she'd let them build a fortress from blankets and cushions off the couch. Hidden in their pretend camp, they whispered and played with stuffed animals.

"I hope you've worked up an appetite," she said. "I've almost got lunch ready."

Noem glanced at his watch. Already past noon, the day was moving on. The scent of the food cooking on the wood-burning stove enticed his empty stomach. "I could use a bite," he said, slipping the timepiece back into his pocket.

"I'll have it on the table in a bit."

"Sounds *gut*." Nodding, he headed into the washroom to clean up. He emerged a few minutes later, ready to tuck into whatever she had prepared. Between making the trip to town for supplies and doing the actual work, he'd skipped breakfast. The cup of coffee he'd fortified himself with had worn off hours ago.

Heading to the sink for a drink of cool water, he couldn't fail to notice the dishes were washed, the counter wiped down and a pretty tablecloth covered the table.

"It looks like it did when *Mamm* was alive."

She smiled. "*Danke.* All it needed was a little attention."

He looked around, admiring her handiwork. Lavinia had scrubbed the kitchen from top to bottom. Everything was in its place, except the drawer sitting on the table. Taken from a large dresser, the bottom was padded with folded blankets.

"Why is that there?"

"It's for Jesse to rest in while I work," she explained.

Admiration filled him. "That's a *gut* idea."

"Learned it from my *mamm*," she commented, laying the *boppli* back in his makeshift bed and checking his diaper. "It helps me keep him close while I'm cleaning."

Noem nodded toward the stove. "And cooking. I'm sorry the appliances are out-of-date. I know you're used to better."

"You forget, I was raised using a wood stove. *Daadi* didn't like propane appliances and wouldn't have them in the house. *Mamm* begged for years, but he said no. I only got them myself when I married Josiah."

"I can't do anything with it," he admitted. "Everything I cook burns or scorches."

"Just a matter of knowing how to spread the coals and where your hot spots are on the top." Satisfied Jesse was fine, Lavinia headed to the old stove. Wiping her hands on a clean dishcloth, she checked the large pot simmering atop the burner. "I believe it's ready," she said, stirring it with a ladle.

Noem tipped back his head. "Smells delicious."

"You're lucky I found enough to put a meal together."

"I didn't even think about getting extra groceries this week," he admitted.

Stepping away from the heat, Lavinia wiped her brow. To help air out the kitchen, she'd thrown open all the windows facing the front of the house. The spring breeze winnowing through the shaded veranda helped chase away the heat.

To keep herself cool, she'd rolled up her sleeves and taken off her flats and hose. Going barefoot didn't seem to bother Amish women, as most rarely wore their shoes when inside. As she'd worked so hard, her *kapp* had gone askew. Her tight bun had also loosened, releasing a tumble of curls. Long silky strands wound their way down her back.

"I guessed as much." She nodded toward a pad and pen on the counter. Her neat handwriting filled an entire page. "I could use some things."

Noem glanced at the list. "I'll get what you need."

"It takes a lot to feed a *familie*."

Looking over her selections, he nodded. Expanding to a six-person household was quite a change. Aside from keeping a few essentials, he and Gabriel rarely ate at home. It was easier to grab a meal at the local café. Neither of them cooked well.

As he'd not had a single minute to restock the pantry, she'd had to make do with the scant offerings she'd found in the icebox. "I can't imagine what you've made since we didn't have much on hand."

Lavinia chuckled. "There was enough for soup. I cut up a few potatoes, an onion and some leftover ham, and then added milk and butter. I seasoned the mix with salt and pepper."

Noem chuckled. "*Mamm* used to call that her 'odds and ends' stew."

"We've all made it when things get a little tight. And there was plenty of cornmeal, so I made a pan of cornbread, too."

"Sounds *gut* to me." Impressed with her thrifty nature, he leaned against the counter. "If you like, we can ride into town later and pick everything up."

Setting the table with cups and utensils, she glanced up. "Why don't you just call it in? Abram can deliver it later. Samuel and Elam promised to help move my things from the old house, too. Elam's got his truck, so you won't have to rent a van."

Noem considered her suggestion. He still

needed to finish painting the washroom Lavinia and the *kinder* would share. If he got straight back to work after lunch, he'd be able to get it done. He'd used a latex wall paint, so he'd only have to go back for touch-ups. As he'd bought plenty, he also planned to freshen the rest of the rooms. The outside, too, could stand a fresh whitewashing. By the time he got finished, the house would be redone from top to bottom.

"It *would* save a trip into town. And I will pay your *bruder* for the use of his truck."

"No need," she said, shaking her head. "They won't take it, and it would be an insult to offer. Whether or not you like it, you're *familie* now. And Muellers always stick together."

Something in her tone revealed her inner tension. Josiah also had relatives in the neighboring town of Haven.

"What about the Simmons clan?"

Gaze dropping, her mouth tightened. "Josiah's people had other thoughts about how things should be taken care of after his passing," she said, speaking in a short, clipped manner.

Curiosity prodded. "Oh?" He recalled Bishop Graber saying Josiah had left Lavinia in a bad way. The sale of the property and house should have generated a tidy sum, but that didn't seem to be the case. Though she had said nothing out loud, he suspected the strain between the Simmons and Mueller *families* was over money.

"It's nothing. Nothing at all." Waving her hands, she shook her head and walked back to the stove. "I don't want to talk about it," she said, ladling soup into two small child-size bowls. "What's done is done."

No reason to push. The details probably weren't any of his business. His *daed* had warned him there was some talk going around about Josiah, but he hadn't given the conversation they'd had much consideration. People gossiped about any little thing, and the facts often got stretched far beyond the truth. Best to let it go. Whatever dealings Lavinia had with Josiah's relatives had left an unpleasant taste in her mouth. He couldn't imagine they'd be so uncaring. Sophie was Josiah's only *kind*. Surely, they would want to see the *youngie* grow up.

Anger can do a lot of things to people.

He could hardly point fingers. His own *familie* had a lot of strife. It was easy to remember how Gabriel had struck Callie's name out of the *familie* Bible after she was excommunicated. Just like that, his only sibling had ceased to exist.

It was disheartening and distressing to witness close relatives turn on one another. Even people who called themselves Christians were prone to negative and destructive emotions.

"If you say so," he replied, closing the matter.

Placing the servings for Penelope and Sophie on the table, Lavinia called into the living room. "Girls, come and eat."

Two disheveled heads popped out of the play tent. Dressed in pinafores and barefoot, both girls were flushed from play.

"Let's get you in your seats." Fetching thick cushions, she placed them on a couple of chairs. She then moved the drawer off the table. Setting it aside, she claimed Jesse from his makeshift bed. "Would you mind?"

"Not at all." Noem helped Penelope into a chair. "There you go."

His niece giggled, one of the first actual signs of joy she'd exhibited since her arrival.

Sophie expectantly lifted her arms. "*Dat*, me now!"

Noem momentarily froze. "Did I hear right?" Grinning, he picked up the little girl. "I think she just called me *daadi*."

Caught by surprise, Lavinia froze. "That's the first time she's said that since Josiah passed."

"We *are* married." Noem put Sophie in her seat. The little girl squealed with glee. "She can call me *dat* if she likes."

"You don't want her to call you *stiefvater*?"

"*Stepfather* doesn't sound very warm." Pausing, he cleared his throat. "I would like to call her my *tochter*. Um, unless you feel it's disrespectful to Josiah's memory."

"I—I don't know."

Mind reeling, Lavinia returned to the stove. Hearing the word *dat* come out of Sophie's mouth rattled her. She wasn't sure why. It was common for *kinder* who had gone through the loss of a parent to connect with a caregiver who reminded them of the lost loved one. Seeing her step into the role of *mamm* for Penelope and Jesse must have triggered a similar response for Sophie. Like Josiah, Noem was a lanky man with blond hair. Mistaking him for her *daadi* during a moment of excitement would be perfectly normal.

But was it something to be encouraged?

Stomach twisting into knots, she began to second-guess her decision to marry Noem. There had been no genuine affection in the deal. Only a fond familiarity.

Uncertainty crept in, preying on her fear of the unknown. Not only was she dependent on the kindness of a man who was practically a stranger, but she'd also come to him with a *youngie* in her arms. Everything she and Sophie were to have would depend on what her new *ehmann* would allow. She had no money of her own. Anything she wanted, she'd have to ask for.

Ruling with an iron fist had enabled Josiah to conceal the state of their finances. She had no idea how much money he made or how he spent it. He'd been able to hide his addiction because she'd never once paid a bill or looked at a bank statement. In theory, the principal was biblically sound. By *Gott*'s design, a man was the head of the *familie* and would manage the household. But the Lord had also cautioned man that he should show his wife understanding and honor her. In accumulating debt, he'd deceived her. And in deceiving her, Josiah had failed to honor her.

"Did I say something wrong?"

Lavinia glanced up. Uncertainty creased his features. *"Nein,"* she said, shaking her head. "I was worried how you would feel taking another man's *youngie* to raise."

"Penelope and Jesse also belong to another man. I intend to raise all three *kinder* as my own."

"Penelope and Jesse are your blood through Callie."

"It takes more than kinship to make a *familie*. If Sophie calling me *dat* disturbs you, perhaps she can use something else."

Forcing doubt aside, she drew in a breath. The devil was certainly doing his work, filling her with all sorts of dire and unfounded speculations. Her life with Josiah had ended. Her marriage to Noem was just beginning. He'd done nothing to make her doubt his sincerity. Learning to trust another man would be hard, but she was determined to try.

"If Sophie wants to call you *dat*, I see no reason to discourage her."

"Then *dat* it is." Offering a tentative smile, he glanced at the pot simmering on the stove. "That smells great." He patted his stomach. "I bet it'll fill this empty spot in my stomach right up."

"I'm getting it on the table as fast as I can." Deftly holding the *boppli* secure, Lavinia nodded toward the larger bowls she'd set out for herself and Noem. "Could you?" she asked, prompting him with a nod. "I've only got two hands, and this little one takes them both."

"Gladly." Ladling out the soup, Noem carried their servings to the table. Returning to the counter, he sliced the cornbread she'd baked and then dished it onto saucers and buttered it up. "Okay?"

"Danke."

After giving Penelope and Sophie each a generous portion, he claimed a chair. "This is a treat. I haven't had a home-cooked meal in ages."

"I hope you like it." Nudging the pot off the heat, she set the lid atop it. "There will be more for later."

Spooning up the thick soup, Noem paused mid-bite. "Aren't you going to eat?"

Lavinia shook her head. Slipping her free hand around Jesse's back, she repositioned him. Hungry, he was beginning to fuss, waving his arms and letting out small grunts of displeasure.

"In a minute. I need to feed the *boppli* first."

One arm flailing, Jesse shoved his free hand into his mouth, gurgling with dissatisfaction. "Um, gaa!"

Claiming the bottle she'd prepared earlier, she sat to feed him. The infant nursed with gusto. "He's such a handful."

Noem broke off a corner of golden cornbread and popped it in his mouth. "I hope you're not regretting your decision."

She lifted her gaze. "I did have doubts," she said, choosing to speak with complete candor. "I was tempted to call off the wedding."

A few lines set themselves into Noem's expression, burrowing around his eyes and mouth. Laying aside his spoon, he reached for a napkin to wipe his mouth. "I have to admit, I thought about backing out, too."

Relief drizzled through her. If they couldn't be honest with each other, there would be no chance of building a real future together. "Did you?"

"*Ja*. Everything happened so fast. My head was spinning."

She grinned. "Mine, too. Sunday morning, I was close to phoning Bishop Graber and telling him to call off the wedding."

"Why didn't you?"

"Because I gave my word," she answered simply. "And I saw a *freund* in need."

Noem laughed. "Desperate need," he added.

"And if I were to be honest, I didn't want to move in with one of my *bruders* or my *schwester*," she confessed.

"Oh?"

"*Ach*, don't get me wrong. I love them all— but not enough to want to live in the homes they share with their spouses and *youngies*." Shaking her head, she halted her words. No reason to keep dwelling on the past.

His gaze traveled to the *boppli* in her arms. Shadows haunted his expression. "I thought about trying to find Erik," he blurted, speaking in *Deitsch* so the little ones couldn't follow the conversation. "Truly, I was tempted."

"Why would you—"

Noem held up a hand. "I didn't because *Gott* commands us to take care of our own. I'm ashamed to say I haven't done that. I know better." He took another bite of the cornbread. After chewing carefully, he swallowed. "I ignored everything around me. I'm at fault for letting the house and property go, too. *Daed* didn't care, so why should I?"

"Death doesn't just touch the departed. It touches us, too. As hard as it is, we must go on living." She looked around. "I remember how it was when Amelia was alive. She always grew such cheery flowers."

Noem's face brightened. "I'd like it to be that way again."

"Best month to start is in April."

"I don't know much about putting in flowers and such. Most I ever did was mow the grass." Expression softening with memory, he chuckled. "*Mamm* banned me from her gardens when I accidentally mistook some of her flowers for weeds and pulled them all up. *Ach*, she was so upset. She told me to stay away from anything green."

"I guess I'll have to teach you which ones are pretty and which ones are pests."

"A vegetable garden would be nice, too. *Mamm* used to grow so much that we hardly ever needed anything from town. And we could put in a few coops and keep chickens. Haven't had them for years. And fresh eggs are always tasty. Maybe even get some meat rabbits. Nothing better than a roasted rabbit's leg with vegetables."

Encouraged by his plans, she smiled. "Been a long time since I've kept rabbits. Be nice to have them again."

A burst of giggles interrupted. Having lost their bibs, both Penelope and Sophie wore splashes of soup on their clothes. Wriggling and kicking their legs at each other, they were ready to run and play.

Hands full with Jesse, Lavinia pushed out a sigh. "If you're finished, go. I'll wash you both up later."

Pushing his chair away from the table, Noem rose. "Let me." He wrung out a rag and helped wipe down messy hands and faces.

Eager to be let free, Sophie wriggled out of his grasp. "No more!"

Penelope followed. With a hop and a skip, they hurried back into the living room. Dropping to their hands and knees, they crawled back into their play tent.

Noem tossed the rag in the sink. "Looks like they are having fun."

"*Ja*. There was a petty squabble over a stuffed

animal, but they got over it." Bottle empty, she set it aside before lifting Jesse to her shoulder.

Noem glanced at the soup she hadn't touched. "You haven't had a bite." He held out both hands. "I can hold him while you eat."

"Danke." Lavinia handed the infant over. Insisting that *kinderbetreuung* was a woman's job, Josiah had rarely taken an interest in tending to Sophie's daily needs. Asking him to feed her or change a diaper was met with a wall of resistance. Noem was a little more flexible and willing to learn. "Just pat him on the back until he lets out a healthy burp. Don't want a *boppli* with a tummy ache."

"I think I can handle that." With awkward hands, Noem pressed his nephew against his shoulder. Since he was unaccustomed to holding a squirming infant, his movements were clumsy.

Jesse immediately fussed, wriggling something fierce even as his little hands turned into fists.

"Ah, goo!" he squalled. His gibberish made no sense.

Patting his diapered bottom, Noem gave him a bounce. "Someone's all bent out of shape."

Breaking off a piece of cornbread to dunk in her soup, Lavinia threw him a glance. "You're doing fine."

Unfortunately, Jesse was not. Opening his mouth, he released a giant burp. And most of his meal.

Noem winced as the warm, damp stream ran down his back, soaking through his shirt. "I don't think I'm doing so great."

Seeing his dilemma, Lavinia grinned. "Welcome to parenthood."

Lifting Jesse, Noem held the *boppli* at arm's length. "How can one little *boi* be so smelly and make so many messes?"

Fat legs kicking the air, Jesse grinned with accomplished glee. "Goo!" he exclaimed, pleased with his handiwork. His diaper sagged with a familiar weight.

Close to panic, Noem sketched a grimace. "What do I do now?"

As she struggled to hold back her laughter, Lavinia's shoulders shook with amusement. Pushing aside her bowl, she rose to help him with the mess. "You pray *Gott* grants you the patience to get them raised."

Chapter Six

Perched on a stepladder, Lavinia slipped a curtain off its rod. Coated in a thin layer of dust and cobwebs, the material was close to disintegrating. Untouched since Amelia Witzel's death, the window treatments should have been replaced years ago.

"Men and housekeeping just don't go together," she muttered.

Unable to salvage the material, she stuffed it in a trash bag. Now that the bedrooms she and the *youngies* occupied had been fixed up and furnished, she'd turned her attention to fixing up the living room. Cleaning every inch, she planned to replace the rugs and curtains, as well as add a few new wall hangings. So that the change wouldn't be too drastic or upsetting to Gabriel, she would remake the window coverings in the style Amelia had favored, using a similar style of material. It wasn't unusual for a new Amish wife to move in with her in-laws. Often, the eldest son took possession of the *familie* homestead, raising his *kinder* in the same house he'd grown up in. Each wife coming after the last was expected to add her individual touch while being respectful to the memory of the woman who had proceeded her.

Though it was a lot of work, none of it deterred Lavinia. Having labored at her *mamm*'s side since she was old enough to walk, she'd learned the value of a woman's place. A man might go out and make the living, but it was the wives and mothers who were the backbone of the home and community.

Instead of resenting it, she embraced it. The Lord knew what He was doing when He gave a man and woman their places on earth. *Kinder, küche, kirche*—which meant children, kitchen and church—was the motto every Amish woman was raised to live by. With so much to do, there wasn't a spare moment for a soul to seek out any trouble. Rising with the sun, she enjoyed putting in a full day. By the time her head hit the pillow at night, she could honestly say she'd spent her time in a worthwhile and fulfilling way that pleased both *Gott* and her *ehmann*. As the Bible commanded, she aspired to live quietly, to mind her own affairs and to work with her hands to keep her home tidy and her *youngies* disciplined. Having lived that way through generations was what allowed the Amish to thrive in a society that was often centered on self.

After taking down the rest of the curtains, she mixed up a vinegar solution to clean the glass panes. She was just about to step back onto the ladder when the sound of tires crunching on the gravel drive interrupted her thoughts. A couple of Gabriel's mongrel hounds set to barking.

She set the bottle and cleaning rags aside. "Now who could that be?"

Neither Noem nor his *daed* was home. After taking a few days to turn his old room into a snug haven for the *youngies*, Noem had set his sights on renovating other parts of the house. They'd not been gone half an hour, so it was unlikely they'd be back so soon. And they'd departed in a buggy, not a gas-powered vehicle.

Hurrying into the nursery, she gave the *youngies* a check. Given lunch, the *kinder* had been put down for a nap. Still sharing a bed, Sophie and Penelope snuggled side by side. Clad in a one-piece sleeper, Jesse was secure in his crib. A gentle spring breeze whispered against the pale-yellow window hangings.

For the time being, all three *youngies* fit.

And while it wasn't unusual for Amish siblings to share a room, there would come a time when they'd need more space. They needed at least five bedrooms. Six would be better, as she'd like to have a place for overnight guests, too.

Leaving the door cracked, she hastened to greet the visitors. Familiar faces came into view as several women climbed out of a large passenger van.

Lavinia looked over the group. Her eldest sister, Annalise, was accompanied by her three sisters-in-law: Maddie, Frannie and Violet. Her middle growing thicker as the months passed, Annalise would soon be adding another *boppli* to her *familie*. Maddie, too, was heavily pregnant with twins.

"I wasn't expecting company."

Annalise waved. "We came to give you an *einweihung.*"

"But I'm not a real newlywed," she corrected with a laugh. "I'm just the *haushälterin.*"

"Nonsense," Frannie countered. "It's just a few things we wanted you to have."

Smoothing her dress and setting her *kapp*, Violet eyed the old house. "I expected better." Married to Rolf, Violet was quite older than the rest of the women. Having narrow eyes and a pinched mouth, she was a dour woman.

Lifting her chin, Lavinia propped her hands

on her hips. The offhanded comment stung. "There's nothing wrong with the house. I rather like it."

"I think it's darling," Maddie said, offering a smile. "The screened-in porch and flower boxes are perfect."

Lavinia glanced at her favorite sister-in-law. A sweet woman hailing from Pennsylvania Amish country, Maddie always had a kind word.

"*Danke*. We're redoing the inside. It looks very nice."

"I like the house, too," Frannie chimed in. "Give it a fresh whitewashing and it'll look brand-new. I know Samuel wouldn't mind lending a hand if Noem needs help."

Lavinia nodded. While all her *bruders* were talented with their hands, Samuel was particularly handy when it came to home improvements. After he'd married Frannie, he'd built his new bride a cabin-style house with his own two hands.

"Elias can help, too," Annalise said, volunteering her *ehmann*. "This very Sunday."

Violet nailed them under a frown. "It is Easter," she reminded. "A time to reflect on our Lord."

"Easter is also a time to spend with our loved

ones," Maddie countered quietly. "And I know Abram won't mind helping out."

Annalise clapped. "And we girls can bring a dish or two. It'll give us a chance to spend time with our new relatives."

Lavinia hesitated. Gabriel wasn't particularly sociable. The old man might not appreciate having the Mueller clan descend for an entire day.

It was on the tip of her tongue to refuse when her thoughts cut a new track. Noem had mentioned it was about time the place had some life in it. Fixing it up was one thing. For a house to become a home, it needed people. Most Amish families were large and lived on each other's doorsteps. Noem and his *daed* would have to get used to the fact that she had a lot of siblings, who would visit often.

"*Ja.* I'm sure Noem would appreciate the help." Having extra hands would make the work go faster. It would also help lighten the incredible load he'd taken on. Anything she could do to help lessen his burden was part of her job. Marriage was supposed to be a partnership, with each spouse contributing equally. The Bible said *Gott* created Eve from Adam's rib. The Lord used a rib because women were meant to stand equally beside men. Not behind or below, but beside them.

If they were going to succeed as a *familie*, then they would have to act like one. Penelope and Jesse would benefit, too. As she intended to treat them as her own, they had handfuls of *tantes*, *onkels* and *cousinen* to meet. They would also learn about Amish traditions and customs that would, hopefully, lead them to join the church when they came of age.

"Then it's a date." Happy she'd gotten her way, Annalise walked around to the back of the van. The *Englisch* driver waited patiently. Opening the back doors, she motioned for the others. "We have presents."

The women gathered the items. The driver was dismissed and would return in an hour. "How are the *youngies*?" Maddie asked as they stepped onto the veranda. "Is everyone getting along?"

"There have been a few snags, but they are doing *gut*. I've put them down for a nap." Lavinia ushered everyone inside.

"I'm glad they are settling in," Frannie said. "I'd worried how Sophie would accept other *kinder*."

Once in the kitchen, Lavinia filled the kettle with water and set it on the stove. It would be impolite not to offer her guests a cup of tea. "She took to Penelope right away, though she isn't as fond of Jesse. She's not sure what to think of a little *boi*."

"And Noem? He treats you well?" Frannie asked.

"*Ja*. I have no complaints. He has been kind to me and Sophie."

Annalise shook her head. "I didn't think you would remarry. At least, not so soon. And not so suddenly."

Lavinia offered a thin smile. "I am certain the Lord knew exactly what He was doing when He inspired Bishop Graber to bring Noem to my door."

"And your relationship…?" Frannie asked, lifting her brows in a certain way.

"Suits us fine," Lavinia finished. "The *kinder* and I have our own rooms and are quite comfortable."

"Then you have no regrets?"

"I wouldn't be human if I didn't have them," Lavinia admitted slowly. "But I am doing as *Gott* commands in Isaiah. 'Remember ye not the former things, neither consider the things of old.'"

"I only want you to be happy," Annalise said.

"Of course," Frannie chimed in. "We all do."

Hearing the kettle whistle, Lavinia lifted it off the stove. Letting the tea leaves steep in the hot water, she set out five mugs. "I am joyful in the Lord's grace and the second chance He has given me," she added. "No woman could ask for more."

The conversation fell to a lull.

Eyeing the bare floors and windows, Violet broke the silence. "I see we caught you in the middle of a task."

Lavinia smiled. "I was about to measure for the new curtains."

"Then you might like this." Grinning, Annalise laid a wrapped parcel on the table. "Open it."

Lavinia wiped her hands on her apron. "You didn't need to. I have plenty from the old house."

"But it's tradition," Frannie insisted. "You must have something new."

Lavinia tore away the brown paper wrapping. Inside was an entire bolt of damask in a shade of ivory. "Oh, my. It's beautiful."

"I know you've had your eye on it. I was going to wait until your birthday, but I thought you could use it now."

"It'll make lovely curtains." Her fingers brushed the fabric. *"Danke."*

Frannie held out her gift. "I got you a set of linens. I know you can always use those."

Lavinia laughed. "Noem was going to take me to buy new things. Now he won't have to."

Maddie, too, had a small gift. "It's not much," she apologized, handing over a framed piece of cross-stitch. Done with a careful hand, a floral pattern circled an old Amish saying: *We gather here with grateful hearts.*

Vision blurring, Lavinia blinked. "It's perfect." She nodded toward a blank space on the wall. "I'll hang it there."

As if saving the best for last, Violet set down a woven basket filled with canning jars. Each was sealed and neatly labeled. "Some of my homemade spiced-apple butter. There's also some vanilla-pear butter and pumpkin butter." A small booklet was also inside.

"Oh, my. These are some of my favorites." Reaching into the basket, Lavinia picked up the handwritten booklet. "What's this?"

"The recipes, as given to me by my *grobmütter,*" Violet said, and her chin quivered more than a little.

Mouth falling open, Lavinia stared at the neatly written pages. Despite many pleas, Violet had staunchly refused to share them. And while many women—including herself—had tried to duplicate them, they'd never quite tasted the same. "I don't know what to say."

"I know you've been wanting to make some yourself." A look of pique crossed Violet's face. "I was selfish to keep them to myself, so here you are. The Lord says we are to be generous."

Lavinia tucked the booklet back into its place. "I'm touched you would offer them to me."

"Why, Violet, I thought we'd have to pry those recipes out of your cold, dead hands," Annalise said behind a bemused grin.

"I know I'd like to have them," Frannie added, and then wagged a finger. "I've begged for ages. Samuel is mad about the vanilla-pear butter. He would eat it on everything if he could."

Suddenly looking uncomfortable, Violet fidgeted in her place. "I know I tend to speak without thinking. I've been praying *Gott* would school my tongue. I meant no offense earlier. I had no right to say anything, given you have lost so much in such a short time."

Feeling the press of tears, Lavinia swiped at her eyes. The friction between the women lessened, lifted by the unexpected olive branch. Known for speaking her mind, Violet rarely apologized.

"We won't speak of anything sad today," she declared, banishing the frown that had taken hold of her mouth. Her losses had been difficult, painful. But the agony had been tempered by many blessings.

The women all smiled and nodded in agreement.

"Amen," they murmured. "Amen."

A brief silence followed.

"I could use a cup of tea," Violet said, hinting that refreshments were yet to be served. "My throat is quite parched."

"I'd take a cup," Annalise added.

Patting her protruding belly, Maddie cocked a brow toward Violet's gift basket. "And I'd love a taste of that apple butter."

Grateful for the support of women she loved and cherished, Lavinia smiled. "And so you shall."

"I'm definitely having the pumpkin butter," Frannie said.

Eager to serve her guests, Lavinia reached for the kettle. Filling the cups, she eyed the fresh loaf of sourdough resting on the counter. Baked that very morning, it waited to be devoured.

"Come, let me slice some bread, and we will enjoy this wonderful gift Violet has shared with us today."

"Nothin's the same," Gabriel grumbled. "Every time I walk in that house, those women have changed somethin' else."

Hoeing a row of weeds growing up the fence line, Noem halted his steps. "Didn't hear what you said."

"I said things are changin' around here," Gabriel retorted. Rake in hand, he pulled the metal tines through the debris filling one of the flower beds. Beneath the old dead growth a few of the heartier annuals lifted their heads. A pile of yard waste, weeds and plants he'd torn out waited to be hauled away in the wheelbarrow. The older man had worked with quiet efficiency, knowing exactly what needed to be done. A few hours later, two of the largest beds bordering the fence were finished.

Ready for a break, Noem lifted his hat to swipe at his perspiring brow. Though the temperature was only in the mid-fifties, he'd worked up a sweat. He had yet to mow the grass. Left untended since the previous winter, the thick grass would be a challenge with man-powered tools. The blades on the mower were dull and would need to be taken off and sharpened.

"*Danke* for offering to lend a hand."

"You're not a gardener," Gabriel grunted. "You wouldn't have known what to pull and what to leave."

"True. I barely know a flower from a weed." Looking over the freshly raked ground, Noem saw some plants had been left in their place. Hearty green stems with bulbous heads poked through the soil, determined to welcome the spring with bright blossoms. Planted years ago, the daffodils returned season after season. Didn't matter that the soil hadn't been tended in ages. Not only had they survived, but they'd also thrived. As Easter was this Sunday, he thought it fitting they would be the first to bloom. Grown by the Amish for the holiday, they were a symbol of rebirth.

"Your *mamm* was the one with a green thumb," Gabriel continued.

Happy to share a pleasant memory, Noem offered a nod. "I remember how the other ladies used to bring her their sick plants. No matter how bad they looked, she could always save them."

"Amelia loved growin' things. She said watchin' a seed grow reminded her of *Gott*'s little miracles, the ones we take for granted." While he spoke softly, Gabriel's face took on an expression of longing. "Lord, how I miss her."

Noem's throat tightened. "I miss her, too."

Pursing his lips, Gabriel looked over his handiwork. "Your *mamm* would have been ashamed I let somethin' she loved go. She'd have expected me to keep things better." Grip tightening on the rake, he glanced around. "House needs paintin'. The fence needs fixin'. Can't believe I let it get this bad. It's like my eyes were closed and I saw nothing except my own misery."

Heart aching over the confession, Noem gave his *daed* a reassuring pat on the back. Offering to help clean up the lawn signaled that Gabriel was accepting the new arrangement. Though he was still distant with Lavinia and the *youngies*, his attitude was beginning to make a change for the better. "No one can blame you. You were grieving. *Gott* would hardly blame you for needing a break."

Kneeling, Gabriel touched one of the daffodils. Though not yet open, the bud would soon unfurl to reveal bright yellow petals. "After your sister left and your *mamm* passed, I doubted *Gott*. I felt nothin' when I read my Bible."

"You aren't alone," Noem confessed. "I've been doubtful, too. But I'm trying to find my way."

"I let my life go," the old man confessed. "And I let my faith go. But I want them back. I want to know joy again. Ecclesiastes reminds us for everything there is a season."

Rubbing his eyes, Noem nodded. "We both need to find our joy. Lavinia… The *youngies*… I know you didn't want them here, but they've bought so much into our lives."

Gabriel glanced up. "Ain't quiet like it used to be, that's for sure," he said, releasing a chuff.

Noem laughed. "Life isn't ever going to be

quiet again. Getting married, raising *kinder*...
I'm in for the long haul."

"I'm proud of you, *sohn*." The old man
tipped his head, squinting in the nearsighted
way that only enhanced the deep lines imprinted around his eyes. "I didn't think you
could pull things together, but you did."

"It wasn't just me. Lavinia's done most of the
work. I'm just doing what she tells me to do."

"The girl's got a *gut* head on her shoulders.
You couldn't have picked better. I like that
she's kept a lot of your *mamm*'s things, without clutterin' up the place with her own."

Noem smiled. "I'm glad you approve."

"Treat her right and you will have a *gut* life."

"I hope so."

Noem knew Lavinia didn't love him. But
he hoped as time went on he could change her
mind. He wanted her to see him as more than
a friend, wishing she would give him the look
of pure adoration she lavished on the *youngies*. But she was still tangled in her feelings
for another man. As Josiah slumbered in a
cold grave, her heart wept for all she had lost.
She was trying to move on, to be strong for
the sake of the *kinder*. In her strength, there
was beauty. A beauty he longed to embrace.
A beauty he longed to call his own.

Not yet. But perhaps someday.

Releasing a loud snuffle, Gabriel swiped at his eyes and nose. "Need to get back to work."

Putting aside his thoughts, Noem offered a nod. "I think we've earned a break. How about we go in and grab a cup of coffee?"

Gabriel eyed the drive, where a handful of buggies were parked. "Don't know if I want to be goin' inside with all those women here."

As the morning wound its way toward noon, a slew of visitors had turned into the driveway. Lavinia's sister and sisters-in-law had shown up, as had a couple of other women he recognized. Though he wasn't close friends with any of them, he knew them well enough from church and other social occasions.

"Lavinia mentioned they'd be working on sewing up some new curtains. You know what that means."

"It means the house is full of hens."

Noem couldn't resist a grin. "No, it means there will be desserts." When visiting, Amish women always had a home-baked treat for the hostess. And women with food in their hands had never hurt any Amish man's feelings. He was perfectly willing to eat anything they cared to bring.

He laid his hoe aside. The fact they'd be hosting Lavinia's *familie* for Easter had spurred him to get busy in the yard, since most of the socializing would take place outside, weather permitting.

Proud of his accomplishment, he pulled back his shoulders. The house was looking like a home again. He was also proud of Lavinia. Instead of complaining, she'd gathered her cleaning supplies and plunged in. She kept a spotless house.

"Now, be nice. Been a long time since we've had any guests. We've not invited a single soul to visit since *mamm* passed."

"Guess I wasn't very welcomin' to anybody, not even my friends," Gabriel conceded.

"Well, times are changing. You're going to go in and you're going to be cordial."

"I see Wanetta Graff's buggy," Gabriel mumbled under his breath as they crossed the yard. "Shoed her horse a few weeks ago." He rolled his eyes. "That old hen will talk your ear off if given half a chance."

"Just listen and smile," Noem advised, opening the veranda's screen door. As he stepped up, a warped board beneath his boot released a squeak. Now that the lumber he'd ordered had been delivered, he had no reason not to replace it. He planned to take care of it soon.

"Umph," Gabriel said, opening the front door and going inside.

Following close behind, Noem walked into

the house. Quite a sight greeted his eyes. The living room and kitchen were a hive of activity. Several women sat at the kitchen table, engaged in measuring, cutting and sewing the new curtains. Others sat on the living room sofa, braiding rag rugs from scraps of material they'd salvaged from old clothes. A few other women kept an eye on the *youngies*, handling the babes with a firm hand. Laughing and chattering, they seemed to be having a fine time.

The group greeted them with smiles.

"Guten tag," Annalise said.

Noem nodded back. Like himself and Callie, there was only a gap of eleven months between the two Mueller girls. At one time he'd briefly considered asking Annalise out after Josiah snapped up Lavinia. However, she only had eyes for Elias Slabaugh and had married him. Together they had two *sohns*. By the look of things, they were due to welcome another *boppli* soon.

"Danke for coming to help Lavinia." Smiling, he looked around. "I've never seen the house look this *gut*." The generosity of her friends and *familie* was truly overwhelming.

An older woman with a plump figure and gray hair glanced up from her sewing. "I see you're making progress with the yard," Wanetta Graff commented.

Puffing up, Gabriel nodded. "*Ja.* A lot is done."

"It'll be lovely when the beds are planted. I remember Amelia's petunias."

Gabriel took off his hat and hung it by the door. "Gonna replant them. As many colors as I can. All around the house. In the flower boxes, too."

Wanetta nodded approval. "Amelia would be pleased."

Tucking his thumbs in his suspenders, Gabriel rocked back on his heels, basking in the attention. "Maybe you'd give me a little advice as to what else to plant."

"I could do that," the older woman countered with a smile. "I do have a few ideas as to what would grow well."

Standing on a stepladder in front of the bay windows, Lavinia slipped one of the new panels over a rod and hung it in its place. "My, it'll be a real showplace when you get finished." Done with the task, she stepped down.

"I'm looking forward to it," Wanetta added. "I'm sure you'll do a fine job."

"You won't be disappointed," Gabriel boasted and added a firm nod. "It'll be the best in town. Maybe even the entire county."

As he listened to the snip of conversation, Noem's brows rose. Years had passed since he'd seen Gabriel have a conversation with any woman outside of his work. Now the old fellow was preening like a peacock showing off its colorful plumage.

Thinking back on the conversation they'd shared, he raised his eyes toward the ceiling. His *daed* had expressed the desire to embrace the renewal of the coming Easter, a resurrection not only of hope but also of his faith.

Forgive my doubt, Lord. Please grant us Your grace to heal this familie.

Chapter Seven

For the Amish, *Gut Freidaag* began at sunup. Lasting until sundown, the day was a period to reflect on their lives and spend time studying the Bible and praying. Because it was a day of fasting, a large meal was eaten the night before. Throughout the day, no work was done, though it was fine to tend to the needs of farm animals. At the end of the fast, which came when the sun disappeared below the horizon, a light supper was permitted. Come Sunday, the house would be brimming with visitors as everyone enjoyed the Easter holiday.

Lavinia rose before the sun Friday morning. Finding her slippers, she reached for her robe. Shivering, she slipped into the warm flannel and belted the ties around her waist to shield herself from the chill lingering in the air. As most Amish houses didn't have central heating, the temperature tended to get a little brisk in the back bedrooms. Though her room had a propane heater, she'd forgotten to turn it on before dropping into bed. She'd stayed warm enough, snuggled under a downy comforter atop a goose-feather mattress.

Yawning and stretching, she hurried into the bathroom for a quick wash. Thankfully the house had hot running water provided by a propane water heater in the well-house. There was also a washer, though clothes still had to be hung on a line to dry. Once cleaned up, she dressed. Then she wound her hair into a tight bun before pinning her *kapp* into place.

Ready to face the day, she peeked in on the *youngies*. Slumbering under the gentle glow of a nightlight, Sophie and Penelope slept soundly. Jesse was awake and beginning to fuss. Hoping to catch him before he began to cry, she tiptoed inside. She lifted him out of his crib, and then placed him on the changing table. Arms flailing, he kicked his chubby legs. Working with quiet efficiency, she got him into a fresh diaper before slipping him into a cute romper.

"Let's go get you something to eat."

Happy to be dry, the *boppli* cooed. "Gaa!" he squealed, wriggling with delight.

"*Ach*, you are a jolly one."

Gazing into his sweet face, Lavinia felt her heart squeeze. *Kinder* were so vulnerable and helpless. Everything *youngies* needed had to be provided by an adult. Neither Penelope nor Jesse had a choice about what would happen in their lives. Losing both parents was a devastating blow, one she'd vowed to soften with kindness and love. They might not be her blood, but that didn't mean she couldn't treat both as her own. The situation they'd all found themselves in wasn't ideal, but she was determined to make it work.

Picking up Jesse, she headed to the kitchen. Expecting to find it empty, she was surprised to see Gabriel. He was clad in his work clothes, his hair styled in the traditional bowl cut most Amish men his age preferred. His beard, bushy and threaded with gray, stretched down his chest.

"Guten morgen," she greeted, determined to be polite and respectful. "I hope we didn't wake you."

The old man glanced up. *"Nein.* I have a few horses of my own to shoe, so I wanted to get an early start." He gestured toward the stove. "Thought I would get it lit for the day."

Shifting Jesse on her hip, she nodded. *"Danke."*

"Glad to do it." Opening the belly of the

beast, Gabriel claimed a bucket sitting nearby. He raked out the ashes, and then stoked the cavity with fresh wood. Adding thin kindling shavings and a few pieces of paper, he struck a match against the iron surface. The match burst into flame, prompting him to toss it inside before he burned his fingers. The makings caught immediately, snapping and crinkling as the fire consumed the dry wood with gusto. That done, he filled the old-fashioned metal percolator with water.

Lavinia's brows rose. Was she imagining things, or was there a shift in Gabriel's demeanor? His usual scowl was missing. "Cleaning it out is my least favorite thing to do," she said to extend the conversation. "The ashes always make me sneeze something fierce."

"Always did it for Amelia," he explained when he'd finished. "She liked wakin' up to a nice warm kitchen and a pot of coffee." After opening a tin, he added a generous scoop of a ground dark roast to the percolator and then set it on the stove. The old metal pot turned plain water into the elixir that made mornings tolerable. As the water boiled and perked, an enticing scent filled the air. A wry twist moved his lips. "Must be quite a change, goin' from a fancy house to this old place."

Lavinia placed Jesse into her daughter's old

high chair. To help Sophie transition into eating like a big girl, Annalise had gifted her with a child-size table and chairs. The girls would use them until it was time to pass them on.

Fussy with hunger, Jesse squirmed.

"Oh, it's not so bad," she answered, filling a bottle with formula. "I grew up using one. And Gran'pa Amos still uses one, too."

Gabriel ran his palm over the simple laminate countertop. "I offered to get Amelia better appliances, but she didn't want 'em," he confessed. "She enjoyed usin' things that gave her a connection with the past. Made her feel more at home."

Sitting down to give Jesse his breakfast, Lavinia popped the bottle in the *boppli*'s mouth. "I like the house. It's snug."

Her words were truthful. Thanks to everyone's hard work, the living room and kitchen brimmed with a comfortable ambiance, harkening back to an earlier, gentler time.

Momentarily descending into silence, Gabriel set out a couple of mugs. "I know I acted ornery the first night you were here," he suddenly blurted out. "I owe you an apology."

She offered a smile. "Not at all. I understand. It's been a challenging time for your *familie*."

Bushy eyebrows knitted. "Difficult... *Ja*. I

couldn't see takin' two *kinder* to raise." Shame-faced, he shook his head. "I was of the mind Callie's *youngies* belonged with their *dat*."

Lavinia tightened her grip on the *boppli*. The idea of Jesse and Penelope being in the care of the man who had walked out on his marriage was unthinkable. She didn't know all the details behind their breakup. But one thing was clear enough: had Erik cared about Callie and their *youngies*, he wouldn't have left his *familie* living in poverty.

"I hope you've changed your mind."

"I have." After lifting the pot off the stove, Gabriel poured two steaming cups of coffee. He carried the cups to the table. "*Gott* has given me a firm shake and opened my eyes."

Well, the Lord certainly does work in mysterious ways.

"I'm glad. And Easter is a time to reflect on His grace and glory."

Having ladled sugar into his cup, Gabriel followed with a splash of cream. "I'm ashamed to admit it, but I turned away from *Gott* after Callie left and Amelia passed. I was angry I'd lost them. It felt like everything I loved was taken away."

Lavinia visually searched the old man's face. Having gone through the grief of losing a spouse, she could empathize with his turbulent emotions. The loss inflicted a deep wound. Given time, it would heal. But the scars it left on the mind and the heart were still painful. The desire to withdraw into solitude was human nature, for the love of another human being was a fragile thing. Bringing immense joy, it could also inflict an unspeakable agony.

"We all go through moments when the days are dark. I know I struggled when Josiah had his accident."

"Aye. I remember hearin' about it."

"Everything happened so quickly. Suddenly, Josiah was gone. The life we'd built together was wiped away. If it weren't for *Gott*, I don't know that I could have gotten through."

Lowering his cup, Gabriel gave her a look. "I don't mean to pry, but some say Josiah left you in a bad way."

Lavinia pushed out a long, deep breath. She was aware that word had gotten around about her financial issues. No one outside her *familie* knew all the details, but that didn't stop folks from wagging their tongues.

"*Ja.* I had to sell the house. Josiah wasn't *gut* with money, and we owed the bank. After I paid the debts, there was nothing left." While not exactly a detailed explanation, it was the truth.

"I'm sorry."

"It is what it is," she countered, refusing to let the past drag her back into an abyss of regret. "My *familie* offered to take me and Sophie in. But I didn't want to be a burden."

"I doubt they would find you a burden," he offered sympathetically.

"Perhaps not. But in my mind, we would be." Feeling compelled to explain, she leveled her gaze with his. "Bishop Graber knew my need when he led Noem to my door."

"Callie would be pleased to know you married Noem," Gabriel said, and a faraway look came into his eyes. "She loved you like a *schwester*."

"I remember the fun we had." Lavinia chuckled. "Like the time you caught us wearing lipstick and eye shadow that we got from an *Englisch* girl."

Gabriel guffawed. "*Ach*, I was so mad. Made you scrub your faces clean."

"We were quite a handful together." The memories were bittersweet, but well worth remembering.

Emotion tightened his expression, regret joining with remembrance. "Once, I prayed *Gott* would take my mind so I wouldn't remember my *tochter*. Now I'm glad I haven't forgotten her and the girl she used to be."

Shifting in her seat, Lavinia cradled Jesse

closer. Relaxed in her embrace, he was safe, warm and comfortable. "Callie will always be a part of our lives. And we will share those memories with her *youngies* when they are old enough to ask about her."

"You are a *gut* woman, Lavinia," Gabriel said, sincere in his compliment. "You have been a blessin' to our *familie*."

Cheeks heating at the compliment, she dropped her gaze. *"Danke."*

Done with his feeding, Jesse began to wriggle. Giving her attention to the infant, she repositioned him on her lap so she could pat him on the back. Belching up a healthy burp, Jesse waved his chubby fists.

Gabriel chuckled. "He's a *gut* eater, like his *onkel* Noem was at that age."

Lavinia angled her head. *"Ja.* He's got a hearty appetite. And if the rest of us want to eat, I need to get busy." Standing, she held the infant out. "Company's coming Sunday, and I've got baking to do. You could help by watching Jesse while I get breakfast started."

The old man looked spooked. "You want me to hold him?"

"Why not?" She set the infant in his lap and guided his hands into the correct position to keep the *boppli* secure. "Now just give him a little bounce on your knee."

Gabriel held tight. "Not sure about this..."

Placed in the hands of a stranger with an unfamiliar face, Jesse gave the old man a wide-eyed look. As his vision focused, a grin split his lips. "Um, awgg!" Squealing with delight, he lunged for the old man's thick beard. Grasping fingers clutched handfuls of gray hair.

"Oh my!" Gabriel exclaimed, working to free his whiskers from the infant's hold. "The *boi*'s goin' to snatch me bald!"

Pleased with his bounty, Jesse refused to let go. "Gawk!" he yelped again, tugging harder.

Amused, Lavinia felt laughter ripple through her. Having discovered his fingers, Jesse had become a master at grabbing and pulling. Driven by curiosity, he lunged at everything he could get his hands on.

"*Ach*, he's got quite the hold on his *poppi*."

The old man broke into a grin a mile wide. His smile extended to his eyes, wreathing his expression in pure delight. "Why, bless his heart. I think the little fella likes me."

Sighing with contentment, Noem pushed his plate away. "I believe that's the best meal I've ever had," he declared, patting his middle. An entire day of fasting hadn't set well with his constitution. The hours had dragged like centuries. His head ached, and dizziness dogged him through the entire day. Chewing on a few aspirins and sipping water had helped, but the ache behind his temple and the blur in his vision never entirely went away. By the time the sun disappeared behind the horizon, he was more than ready for a meal. It didn't help matters that Lavinia had spent the afternoon creating a variety of delicious dishes, each one more enticing than the last. The chicken and dumplings she'd made smelled wonderful, and the chocolate cake with thick frosting looked delightful.

"Best I've ever had," Gabriel agreed, forking up his last bite of cake and swallowing it down.

Lids fluttering, Lavinia returned a shy smile. "*Danke*. I'm glad you liked it."

Noem grinned. He'd always been happy to sit down at the dinner table but had recently slowed down on his consumption. Eating out all the time had grown tedious. He'd rather skip a meal than consume yet another platter of greasy fried food from the local café. Not anymore. Lavinia was an excellent cook. She'd also found his *mamm*'s recipe box. The cake she'd baked was a Witzel favorite, complete with fudge icing. A single piece wasn't enough, so he'd helped himself to another.

"If I'd known you could cook this *gut*, I would've jumped in line in front of Josiah years ago," he declared.

Amusement tugged at the corners of Lavinia's mouth. "If I'd known I married a man with a hollow leg, I would've made a bigger cake."

"Somethin' about it was different," Gabriel commented, scratching his temple. "Can't figure out what, but it tasted better than Amelia ever made it."

"It's the sour cream. I always add a few good dollops."

"Never would have guessed that would taste so *gut* in a cake."

"Learned it from one of the ladies in my sewing circle." Pushing away from the table, she gathered the dishes. "Believe it or not, I was a terrible cook when I married Josiah. I couldn't boil water without burning it."

Noem rose to do his part. "I wouldn't believe it." He'd taken to helping around the house, doing the chores that would ease her burden. Until he'd lived with *youngies*, he'd never had any idea how much work it took to keep three babes clean and fed. Not only did Lavinia have Jesse constantly at hand, but Penelope and Sophie were active the moment their eyes popped open in the morning. Mobile and curious, they were into everything. To keep them entertained and teach them the value of work, they'd been given simple tasks to accomplish each day.

Imitating the adults, Penelope and Sophie carried their dishes to the sink.

"Danke," Noem said, dunking them into steaming-hot water.

Lavinia wrung out a dishrag. "Now wipe up your table," she instructed, handing it to Penelope. She looked at Sophie. "And put your chairs in place."

The girls obeyed, completing their jobs as best little people could.

"I did it!" Penelope grinned, holding up the rag.

"Me first!" Sophie cried, pushing the chairs against the table.

"You've got a *gut* hand with them," Gabriel observed. "They are well-behaved."

"Oh, they try my patience." After washing and rinsing each dish with care, Lavinia stacked them on the drying rack. "They aren't always angels."

Determined not to be left out of the activities, Jesse fussed, kicking his legs and waving his arms. "Awk!" he screeched, tossing away the teething ring he'd drooled on.

Retrieving the item, Gabriel chuckled. "Now, now, little man, let's not get testy." To lend a hand, he plucked Jesse out of his high chair. The infant was beginning to sample solid foods. Rather than relying on store-bought selections, Lavinia created her own. Almost every ingredient she used was all-natural and organic.

Now that the ice had thawed, Noem's *daed* had taken a shine to his firstborn *enkel*. Gabriel dandled Jesse on his knee, making funny faces and noises. The *boppli* was thriving with all the extra attention and affection.

I never would have believed it if I hadn't seen it with my own eyes.

Having taken the house in hand, Lavinia made sure her domain was spick-and-span. From her point of view, there was a place for everything, and everything should be where it belonged.

Noem looked at his *ehefrau*. As usual, she struggled to keep the thick strands of her hair pinned under her *kapp*. Stray curls were always sneaking out, winding around the nape of her neck. She often brushed them away from her rosy cheeks with a distracted hand, unaware of how enticing those curls were.

Pushing out a sigh, he reluctantly pulled his gaze away. He would have given anything to let down her hair and touch the silken strands.

There was only a single fly in the ointment.

They were wed, but they weren't husband and wife. His heart longed for a deeper connection with the woman he'd married.

But living together for less than a week didn't make a relationship. True, they shared a common past and three *youngies* between them. But they didn't know each other as mature adults. Years had passed since they'd socialized, and he'd always been on the periphery of her friendship with Callie. The girl he remembered had grown into a woman and a *mutter*. Her life experience far surpassed his. In a way, he felt stunted, left behind. He'd always been the odd man out, the guy who stuttered and blushed like a fool around a pretty girl.

His *daed* had told him the secret was in doing the small things. Making a woman feel valued, secure and loved was key.

Snagging a towel, Noem dried the dishes and returned them to their place in the cabinet. Before he'd married Lavinia, dirty dishes would sit in the sink for days before getting washed up. His clothes, too, were more likely to land on the floor than in the hamper, and things were scattered willy-nilly, left where they were dropped. Now he took care to tidy up after himself. So did his *daed*. They were no longer two single men living like pigs in a sty. The house was neat, well organized and comfortable. And he liked it that way.

She gave him the side-eye. "Aren't you a helpful one?"

"You did all the cooking. The least I can do is put them away."

"Can't say I don't appreciate it."

"The sooner it's done, the sooner we can sit down and have a little rest. You've been on your feet all day."

"You know what they say," she returned, dunking a final pot into the soapy water and wiping it down before rinsing away the bubbles. "A man works from sun to sun, but a woman's work is never done."

"Aye, true enough." He'd cleaned and raked within an inch of his life, but once the repairs were done, there wouldn't be much to do past the upkeep. And after he went back to work, he'd be gone most of the day, as would Gabriel. Both had jobs in town and departed soon after the sun rose. Most days they weren't home until well into the evening.

Once they returned to a regular schedule, Lavinia would be home alone all day. Making a living wasn't half as hard as keeping a house. He admired the way she ran everything on schedule, juggling her cooking, cleaning and *kinder* with an efficiency that bordered on precision. Rising early, it was nothing for her to have Jesse on her hip, two little girls under her feet and still manage to get a meal on the table without blinking an eye. In the evenings she would work on her mending and other sundry chores. After putting the *youngies* down to sleep, she would give an hour to the Lord, reading her Bible and jotting her daily devotional in the journal she kept. By the time she retired, the hour was late.

Done with the dishes, Lavinia wiped her hands on a towel before hanging it to dry.

"It's what the Lord intended. The Bible says a woman should work with willing hands. It pleases Him for us to live by His word."

Noem dropped his gaze. Baptized at eighteen, he'd made a vow to live by the word of *Gott*. However, over time as his circumstances shifted in his life, he found himself drifting further and further away from the teachings in the Bible. He attended church on Sunday, listened to the minister's sermons—and then promptly set the lessons aside once the service had ended. From his point of view, spending three hours sitting in the pews was quite enough time to give. Nor did he believe himself to be a bad Christian for doing so. He wasn't a liar, a cheat or a thief. Surely the Lord wouldn't judge him badly for being a bit inattentive.

That was going to have to change. He'd married a woman who was strong in her faith. Lavinia made it a point to make *Gott* part of her daily life. To keep herself in the word, she often sang hymns of praise as she worked, filling the house with her melodic voice. She sang slightly off-key but made up for her lack of talent with enthusiasm. When she wasn't singing, the radio in the kitchen was tuned to a local station that played a mix of gospel music and uplifting sermons. Because Humble was primarily an Amish settlement, a few hours a day were devoted to Amish events and news throughout the community. The station hosts also played afternoon Bible programs for *youngies* that Penelope and Sophie listened to with rapt attention. The *Ordnung* allowed the use of the device because it was an important safety feature during times of harsh weather or other emergencies.

"You're right. *Gott* expects better of me, and I've let Him down."

"I could say the same," Gabriel added.

Kitchen spotless, Lavinia reached for Jesse. Having done their simple tasks, Sophie and Penelope had sprawled on a rug in the living room, dumping their crayons on the floor to scribble in their coloring books.

"*Gut Freidaag* is a time for new beginnings," Lavinia said. "I say we make it a point to have a Bible reading after supper. Not just the adults, but the *youngies*, too."

Gabriel brightened. "I'd like that."

Leaning back against the counter, Noem gazed around the comfortable dwelling. The foundation of the Amish community was firmly rooted in obedience to *Gott*. Serving the Lord wasn't just done through reading the Bible. It was done through living by His commands, turning words into actions throughout one's daily life.

It's time to leave my careless ways behind.

Embracing his faith meant he'd be taking one step closer to the man *Gott* meant for him to become: an *ehmann* to Lavinia and a *vater* to the *youngies* he'd taken to raise.

Chapter Eight

Come Easter Sunday, the house was full to the brim. Almost every member of the Mueller familie had arrived to enjoy a day filled with food, fellowship and fun.

Taking command of her kitchen, Lavinia kept a close eye on the pies she'd popped into the oven.

"Twenty more minutes," she murmured, reminding herself not to let them burn even as she directed the other women where to set the food they'd prepared for the potluck. The countertops overflowed with homemade delicacies. Each woman had contributed her signature dish, which would, in turn, be devoured by hungry men.

As the men were unwilling to sit idle, they'd pitched in to help with the larger repairs that needed to be done outside. Having shown up with his tools in his buggy, Samuel had replaced a few rotting boards on the veranda. Rolf had helped, prying away the old wood and carrying in replacements. Abram was also skilled with a hammer, so he and Noem worked to reset loose posts and mend the broken pickets on the fence. Elam had volunteered to give the house a *gut* whitewashing. He'd brought some of his *Englisch* friends to help, and the work progressed at a steady pace. Gabriel tilled the soil in his flower beds. Excited about bringing them back to life, the old man chattered away with Wanetta Graff about the flowers he'd selected. He'd also begun to lay out a vegetable garden and looked forward to the time when he could start sowing the seeds.

The *youngies*, too, were engaged in a project of their own. While the Amish didn't have any belief in the Easter Bunny, they still participated in activities like coloring eggs. And though they didn't have a dedicated church service for the event, there would be a prayer session later to give thanks to *Gott*. A minister, Abram would deliver the sermon.

Satisfied all was on schedule, Lavinia poured herself a fresh cup of coffee from the pot brewing on the stove. Her feet ached from standing all morning. She longed to sit down and have a break. But there was too much to do. Up at dawn, she'd hurried to get herself and the *kinder* ready to greet company. She took a sip of the caffeinated brew and released a sigh.

"A penny for your pondering," Annalise said, jarring her thoughts.

"Is that all they're worth?"

"You tell me."

"Just thinking about the changes in my life. My head's still spinning. I've barely had a minute to catch my breath."

Annalise frowned. "I know you were pressed because the house sold. But you always had a place to go. You know that. You didn't have to marry Noem. My spare bedroom was always open to you and Sophie."

Returning to the stove, Lavinia topped off her coffee. The percolator was running empty, so she discarded the dregs and set a fresh one to brewing.

"I could have stayed with *familie*. But it's not what I wanted."

"You're braver than I am." Annalise shook her head. "Taking on an *ehmann* and two little ones on short notice."

"I did it for Callie. Her life turned out so badly, and she didn't seem to know how to fix it. And Noem needed someone, so it's been *gut* for both of us."

"I know it's customary, but I'm not as adventurous as you. I couldn't jump right into the unknown like that."

Grabbing an oven mitt, Lavinia peeked into the stove. The pies were beginning to take on a golden hue, indicating they'd soon be ready. As she couldn't decide between apple and cherry, she'd made both. Rolf's eldest son, Henry, sat outside, cranking the old-fashioned ice cream churn. When he finished, there would be homemade vanilla ice cream. For those who preferred a savory pie, she'd sliced up some sharp cheddar cheese.

Satisfied, she closed the oven door. "Don't think I didn't look at all the options. I did consider how it would affect Sophie, too."

"How has she taken the move?"

"*Gut.* She and Penelope are close, though she isn't sure what to think about a *boppli.* And she likes Noem. She calls him *dat* now."

"Oh?"

"*Ja.* A little jarring when she first did it. But Noem is her stepfather."

"Makes sense." Squinting, Annalise gave her a close look. "How are you adjusting?"

Lavinia glanced around. "I'm settling in. I won't say it's been easy. We've hit a few snags."

"Like?"

"Mostly just getting to know each other

again. We were friends, but we haven't been close since Callie left. He's changed. And so have I."

"Well, you'll certainly get to know him since you live under the same roof."

"I used to think so, but I've found that's not entirely true." Pulling in a breath, she went on to explain. "I dated Josiah for two years and was married to him for seven. I thought I knew him. But it turns out I didn't."

Realizing she'd hit a sore spot, Annalise reached out and laid a hand on her arm. "*Ach*, forgive me. I didn't mean to bring back a bad memory."

Lavinia reached for her *schwester*'s hand and offered a reassuring squeeze. "Josiah was a *gut* man in a lot of ways. I wish he had asked for help, but he chose not to. What he did was wrong, but I can't keep blaming him for everything I lost. Instead, I choose to leave him in *Gott*'s hands. I also praise the Lord for everything I have gained."

"You always were strong in the faith," Annalise murmured.

"I pray *Gott* will bless this union and this household."

Stepping back, Annalise looked around. "The Lord must be doing His work. It's been years since I've seen a smile on Gabriel's face.

Since we're in different church districts, I only ever saw him around town. He always looked so dour."

"He lost so much. First Callie went under the *bann*, and then Amelia passed. And then Callie died before they could make any amends. He was truly heartbroken."

"You wouldn't know it today." A mischievous grin lit Annalise's pretty features. "I dare not think it, but it seems to me he might be taking a shine to Wanetta."

"Wanetta and Gabriel?" A giggle slipped past Lavinia's lips. "Now that would be quite a match."

"Why not? They are both widowed."

Lavinia mulled over the idea. Just as the Amish had *familie* formation marriages, they also encouraged companionship marriages, which were usually between older folks who'd finished raising their *youngies*. Gabriel and Wanetta would fit perfectly together. Not only did they share a common background, but they'd also known each other for decades and were around the same age. Amelia Witzel and Wanetta had also been best friends.

"It would be a *gut* match...if we could get them to agree."

"There's always hope," Annalise agreed.

A loud cry interrupted the conversation.

Glancing into the living room, Lavinia saw Maddie struggling to lift Jesse from the playpen where the little ones had been put down for naps. Her protruding stomach was so large she had trouble bending over while keeping her balance. Frannie hurried to help Maddie catch her balance before she tipped over.

"Have a care. You just about fell."

Regaining her footing, Maddie cradled her huge belly. "I'll be okay. All that kicking inside threw me off for a minute."

"Are the babies awake?" Hurrying over, Annalise held out a hand. "May I?"

"Of course." Reaching out, Maddie guided Annalise's palm to her belly. "Right here."

Palm pressed flat, Annalise smiled. "Oh, my. They are kicking up a storm. You're carrying low, so I am betting these are both *bois*. Going to be active ones, too." Laughing, she indicated her thickening middle. "I've got Zeke and Eli so I'm hoping for a girl this time."

Eyes rimmed with dark circles, Maddie offered a nod. "Abram would be thrilled with *sohns*, though I have to admit I'd be happy with *mädchen*, too."

Joining the women, Lavinia picked up Jesse. Arms and legs flailing, he'd set to bawling. It wasn't hard to guess he'd soaked his diaper.

"I know Abram can't wait. How's Josh handling the idea?"

Maddie's expression brightened. "Josh is excited, too. He can't wait." Though Josh belonged to her twin, Maddie had taken her nephew to raise after her *schwester*'s tragic death when the child was just a toddler. And with the *boi*'s *vater* in prison for life, Abram had legally adopted him.

Lavinia gave her *schwägerin* a fond smile. She'd liked Maddie from the beginning. Abram had met her at the *familie* market and had fallen head over heels that same day. Despite the obstacles between them, he'd set his cap and went after the woman who'd claimed his heart with her gentle manner. Having passed their first anniversary, they were excited about welcoming their *kinder*.

Hearing Jesse cry, the other infants started wailing.

Throwing out a sigh, Frannie claimed her child. Hearing the commotion, Violet hurried out of the nursery. Her toddler, Hannah, had needed a change of clothes after Penelope had dumped a cupful of bright purple food coloring all over her. For her transgression, Penelope had been put in time-out. Sitting in a corner facing the wall, she moaned about the fun she was missing.

So the *youngies* wouldn't make a mess in the house, they'd been sent outside to the veranda to color eggs for the hunt. Rolf and Violet's *tochter*, Trisha, was to supervise the younger ones, but it hadn't worked out well. Now a teenager, Trisha was pouting about having to help babysit. Hiram and Hershel, who belonged to Samuel and Frannie, had eaten more eggs than they'd colored. Annalise's *bois* and Maddie's *sohn*, Josh, had decided to see how far boiled eggs would travel with their slingshots. After hitting the side of the freshly painted house, they'd promptly gotten their slingshots taken away by their *onkel* Elam. Sophie ran back and forth, sneaking Penelope a pink egg she'd filched.

"This isn't fun," Trisha moaned, dragging her feet across the living room before throwing herself onto the sofa. "Coloring eggs is for babies."

Violet nailed her oldest child with a frown. "*Gott* says to do all things without grumbling. I suggest you find something else to do to make yourself useful."

Holding the sopping *boppli*, Lavinia cocked her head toward the kitchen. "Maybe you could check on my pies while I change Jesse."

Rolling her eyes, Trisha rose to her feet. "I hate doing girl things," she grumbled. "I'd rather be outside building and working like the *bois* get to do."

"Then go ask Elam if you can lend a hand with the painting," Violet said, pointing toward the door.

"I will!" Mouth stretching into a grin, Trisha clapped and raced out the door.

Lavinia watched her niece go. "What's that all about?"

Violent threw her hands up. "It's called fourteen. Too old to be a kid, and too young for *rumspringa*." She gave her youngest a fond glance. "I'm glad Hannah is still quite a few years from that age. They grow up so fast."

"*Ja.* If only they could stay little," Frannie agreed.

"I have to admit I'm ready for Jesse to be out of nappies," Lavinia said, heading toward the nursery. "Someone check my pies, please!"

"I will," Frannie offered, heading toward the kitchen.

Leaving the commotion behind, Lavinia laid Jesse on the changing table.

Proud of his accomplishment, he grinned with glee. "Bleck!" he gurgled, kicking his arms and legs. As he was learning to crawl, he was anxious to explore. Soon he would be going at top speed. When that happened, she'd have a hard time keeping up.

"My, aren't you a jolly one?" she said, reaching for a pack of wipes and a fresh diaper.

Every time she gazed at his sweet face, her heart swelled with love…and longing. She'd wanted more little ones. Desperately. True, she had her hands full with three. But that didn't stop the ache to fill her arms with another *boppli*.

Now twenty-five, she knew her biological clock was ticking. She was of an age when having more *kinder* was possible. But that would mean a change to her relationship with Noem. A restructuring of the terms of their deal was within the realm of possibility. If only she dared to let him in.

Am I ready?

She wasn't sure what the answer should be. Josiah's lies had destroyed her trust. It would take a lot of time and healing to repair the damage.

A breath like a sob suddenly broke from her lips. She should be in love with the man she'd vowed to stay with for a lifetime.

But she wasn't.

Pressing a hand to her forehead, she let her eyes fall shut. It was no way to live, nor did she want to.

Having pried off another broken picket, Noem reached for one of the brand-new replacements piled nearby. Setting it in place, he hammered in a couple of nails. Satisfied with his work, he stepped back.

"That's the last one." Lifting his hat, he wiped his perspiring brow.

Abram Mueller nodded. "I've reset all the loose posts, so it should stay in place for quite a while."

"*Gut,*" Noem agreed. "Looks brand-new. All it needs now is a coat of paint."

Abram jerked a thumb toward his youngest sibling. Having worked all morning painting the house, Elam and his friends were finishing up the trim around the doors and windows. "Elam and his buddies can get to it after lunch," he said, giving his pocket watch a check. "It's nearing noon, so I'm sure they're ready for a break."

Glancing over at the busy men, Noem felt his throat tighten with emotion. He'd known they would be entertaining Lavinia's relatives for the day, but he did not know what the Mueller clan had planned. Arriving early with their supplies, the men had gone straight to work. But that was the Amish way. If they saw something that needed to be done, they did it. If a neighbor needed a hand, they lent it.

"I can't thank your *familie* enough for the help."

After gathering his tools, Abram walked

across the gravel drive. Buggies parked, the horses munched contentedly on their feed bags. "You are *familie*," he said and looked over the edge of his black-framed glasses. "And the work needed to be done."

Noem stacked the extra pickets in a small shed beside the barn, then stowed away his hammer and nails. "I'm ashamed we let the place get run-down. I know it disappointed Lavinia when she arrived. I could see it in her face that she expected better. I had no business asking her to marry me and then moving her into such a mess. I promise, she will have a bigger house. As soon as I can manage it."

Abram cocked his head. "Lavinia's not the kind to complain about what her *ehmann* provides."

Noem laughed. "I was expecting an earful, but she hasn't uttered a single word. She's done so much with so little."

Rolf ambled up, catching the tail end of the conversation. A big, heavy-set fellow, his stride was double that of most men. Despite his size, he was known to be a gentle giant.

"Whatever you give a woman, she will make greater," he countered with a chuckle. "They are far superior, and they always will be."

"I've no doubt. In just a day, she and her sewing circle whipped up new curtains. And most everything that doesn't move has been dusted or scrubbed within an inch of its life. I don't think it was this spotless when my *mamm* was alive."

"Lavinia runs a tight ship," Rolf said and gave him a clap on the shoulder with a friendly hand. "You and the *kinder* will be all hands on deck."

All true. While an Amish man might consider himself the head of the household, it was the woman who managed the home. Because the home was the center of Amish life, a wife's role in maintaining it was of the utmost importance. No man worth his salt made a single decision without the support and advice of his better half.

"I am thankful Bishop Graber matched us."

"I have prayed for *Gott* to bless your marriage," Abram said.

"We all have," Rolf added. "And the Lord promises we shall again find joy in our grief."

"*Danke*. So many *gut* things have happened since she came." Noem glanced toward the yard where Gabriel stood with Wanetta. The two were deep in conversation, marking out the flower beds and vegetable garden with the flowers and produce that were yet to be planted. "It's been a long time since I've seen

Daed talk like that. It was getting to where he wasn't speaking much at all."

"I'm glad to see him smiling again," Abram said as they crossed back toward the house.

Noem pushed open the gate, pleased that the hinges no longer squeaked. Grass cut and raked, the yard offered a pleasant place to gather and socialize. Several large trees planted near the perimeter of the fence offered a shady place to rest and relax. Picnic-style tables had been set up for lunch, as had several benches and folding chairs. A variety of drinks waited to be served, including pitchers of lemonade and iced tea. A cooler filled with bottled water and other soft drinks also beckoned the thirsty workers. The women hurried back and forth, rounding up the *youngies* even as they prepared to bring out the food.

"We're almost ready to eat," Frannie called. Annalise spread a large quilt out on the grass for the younger *kinder* to lounge on.

With their tools put down, the men used the garden hose to wash up. A bar of homemade soap was handed around. Lathering up, Noem cupped his hands under the stream. Bending over, he applied the suds to his face, scrubbing the stubble he'd let grow.

"Looks like you've got a *gut* start there,"

Samuel said, handing over the towel they all shared.

Noem rinsed his face and accepted the offering. A week's worth of stubble wasn't much. As it was, he looked scraggly and unkempt.

"Can't say I like it," he admitted, pressing the cloth against his face. "All the darn thing does is itch. I'm tempted to reach for my razor."

Using his fingers to smooth his long beard, Samuel laughed. "That'll pass when you get some real growth. Once you get used to wearing one, you won't think twice."

"I am glad the *Ordnung* allows us to clip them down." Those who worked in occupations like welding found it to be a useful safety measure. Others preferred the look of a shorter style.

Rubbing a hand against his bare face, Elam Mueller laughed. "Ain't planning to stay Amish, so I don't have to grow one if I marry."

Rolf shot his youngest sibling a look. "It's your choice. But you haven't got no place poking fun at those who do."

One of Elam's friends reached out, giving Elam's cheek a few light taps. "Look at that baby face. Couldn't grow a beard if he wanted."

Elam swatted the air. "I could grow a beard if I wanted," he groused. "*Englisch* guys can wear them, too."

The men all laughed. Most Amish men wore their beards with pride, signifying their commitment to their *Gott*, their kinfolk and their community.

"You might yet change your mind about being baptized," Abram said. "The Lord can do mighty powerful things."

Elam laughed. "I won't say it couldn't happen."

"I will pray it does."

Laughing and teasing each other, the men finished washing up. Hands and faces clean, they joined the women and *kinder*. Everyone gathered around, ready for a well-deserved meal.

Searching through the group, Noem looked for Lavinia. Her attention was tied up with the *youngies*, getting them ready to eat. Violet kept up with the infants, corralling them in a shaded playpen. Wobbling on his hands and knees, Jesse was determined to make a break for freedom.

Ready to eat, the men lined up. Accepting a plate from Abram's wife, Noem scanned the buffet. The women had outdone themselves with a feast fit for a king. Dutch cabbage rolls, chicken potpie and roast beef were some of the main courses. Sides included mashed and baked potatoes, coleslaw, and cheese noodles.

Dessert included pies, cakes and ice cream. Home-churned butter, fruity jams and honey harvested from the beehives waited to be spread across thick slices of bread and biscuits. Almost everything was made from homegrown gardens and farm-raised livestock.

"I don't know where to start." Claiming a fork, he stabbed a few slices of roast beef. Then he dipped into the mashed potatoes and drizzled brown gravy on the top. After adding a few other sides, he walked to a nearby table and sat.

Humbled, Noem glanced toward the sky. Though the day had dawned with a bit of a chill, the afternoon had warmed to a tolerable temperature. While working hard, almost every man had discarded his jacket and rolled up his sleeves. The sun sent out rays of bright warm light. A gentle spring breeze winnowed through the trees. Overall, it was a perfect day to thank *Gott* for the gift He'd given mankind.

Plate in hand, Lavinia sat down across from him. Abram and Maddie joined them.

"Mind if we sit?" Abram asked, nodding toward a space on the bench.

Noem scooted over. "Not at all."

Arms circling and supporting her large belly, Maddie sat down beside Lavinia. "Not sure I'll fit," she laughed. "My stomach sticks out enough to make a table all its own."

Lavinia gazed fondly at her sister-in-law. "I remember carrying Sophie. Such a joy to feel a new life growing."

Maddie placed her palm against her belly. "I agree. It's a wonder the first time you feel that little flutter inside." A wince crossed her face. "But I could certainly do without that kicking against my ribs at night."

"Not going to be a lot of sleep for us when they're born," Abram said, laughing. "They seem to be night owls and like to do their wrestling after sundown."

"And I'm loving every minute of it," Maddie returned, offering a shy smile. "There will be time to sleep when I'm old and gray. For now, I want to enjoy every minute I can."

"They grow so fast," Lavinia agreed. "Blink your eyes and they will be teenagers next."

"Are you and Noem planning to have more?" Maddie asked.

Blushing, Lavinia dropped her gaze. "We haven't decided," she murmured, appearing to distance herself from the awkward question by spreading a napkin across her lap. "It is entirely in *Gott*'s hands."

Caught short by the innocent inquiry, Noem felt warmth spread across his face. Most everyone knew their marriage was one of convenience. When he'd agreed to a platonic relationship, he'd believed he would be satisfied with their agreement.

But he wasn't.

He also didn't believe Lavinia was happy. Looking at her, he saw dark circles under her eyes and the slight downward slant haunting the edges of her mouth. Though she often smiled, her gaze was distant. And when she looked at him, the merriment she gave others never truly extended toward him. For the sake of appearances, she was only pretending to be content.

It's time to change that.

For that to happen he would have to do more than provide a home.

He would have to win her heart.

Chapter Nine

The day had finally come to its end. Following lunch, Abram preached a short sermon touching on *Gott*'s sacrifice and gift to mankind. Afterward, everyone took a turn sharing what the significance of the Lord's resurrection meant on a personal level. They'd then sung a closing hymn, sending words of praise into the clear sky.

The rest of the afternoon was devoted to activities to entertain the *youngies*. Most everyone participated in a variety of games, which culminated in an egg hunt before sundown. Aside from a few squabbles and one scraped knee, the events had gone off without a hitch. The hour was late when the last guests departed.

Overall, Lavinia viewed the day as a success. Noem had gotten on well with her siblings and their spouses. He'd also done his best to make friends with the *youngies*, playing with as much enthusiasm as an adult could muster. For a man who hadn't spent a lot of time around *kinder*, he was adjusting to the demands of parenting. He'd helped Sophie and Penelope with their baskets, making sure the older *bois* didn't outpace the younger girls in their enthusiasm to claim the most eggs. And her heart had almost melted when he'd picked both girls up and carried them into the house. Plump arms wrapped around his neck, they'd rested their heads on his shoulders, trusting him to get them safely inside.

The biggest surprise came from Gabriel. Not only was he welcoming, but he'd also smiled through the entire day. While he'd given everyone a kind word, most of his attention was directed toward Wanetta. Sharing an interest in gardening, they'd made plans to visit local greenhouses to shop for plants. It wasn't exactly walking about, but it was a beginning.

"It's *gut* to see *Daed* enjoying himself," Noem commented as he helped put the *kinder* down for the night. Concentrating with due diligence, he tried to keep Jesse still as he changed the wriggling *boppli*'s diaper.

"Gak!" Shrieking, Jesse kicked his legs and waved his arms.

Getting Sophie into her pajamas, Lavinia glanced up. "Sounds like he's not ready to be put down."

"Come on, little man," he grumbled. "Be still."

Legs pumping at top speed, his nephew let out another piercing squall.

"Now, Jesse, be good for your *onkel*." Gritting his teeth, Noem got the infant changed.

Lavinia tucked Sophie in beside Penelope. "Say your prayers before you sleep."

Pressing their hands together, the girls bowed their heads.

"'Now I lay me down to sleep,'" she began, guiding them through the words. "'I pray the Lord my soul to keep…'"

Remembering the rest, Penelope finished, "'May *Gott* guard me through the night, and wake me with the morning light.'" A grin lit her face at her accomplishment.

"Very *gut*." Bending, Lavinia gave each girl a peck on the cheek. "I'm so proud of you."

Having won the battle with Jesse, Noem dressed his nephew in a onesie. "Finally done."

Lavinia smiled at him. "You're getting the hang of it."

"I don't know why he's so fussy." Leaving the changing table, Noem laid Jesse in his crib.

The *boppli* immediately pressed his hand into his mouth and gnawed at his fingers.

Noticing his distress, Lavinia slipped her thumb between his lips, pulling down to expose his gums. A bare sliver of white poked through the soft pink surface. "He's teething. Looks like his first tooth has broken through."

Noem grinned. "That's *gut*, right?"

"He's developing on time."

"Wow. Teeth." He shook his head. "He'll have a full set soon."

"*Ja*, he will." She placed her palm against Jesse's forehead. "He's got a little fever, too."

"Should we take him to the doctor?"

"*Nein*. It's to be expected." Lavinia moved to the dresser where she kept the baby supplies on hand and opened the top drawer. "I'll give him some medicine to help with the discomfort and bring down his temperature."

Noem eyed the bottle. "Is that okay?"

"It will help him sleep." She opened the bottle and filled a dropper with the correct amount. Unlike older Amish women who relied on home remedies, she preferred over-the-counter medicines when tending to the *youngies* and their various ailments. The *Ordnung* did not restrict anyone from seeking medical care. Many Plain folks in the community used local doctors and pharmacies and went to the hospital as needed.

After administering the medicine, she rechecked the crib to make sure Jesse would sleep safely. Satisfied, she tucked him into his sleep sack. Dimming the lamps throughout the room, she motioned for Noem to follow her into the living room.

"Jesse should be all right for now," she said and stifled a yawn. "I'll check him in thirty minutes to make sure he's resting."

Noem gave her a hard look. "You were up before the sun. You should get some rest. I can stay up awhile longer and look in on him."

Aching from head to toe, Lavinia mulled his suggestion. The chance to unwind enticed. "*Danke.* I would like to wash up if you don't mind keeping an eye."

"Not at all." Noem headed toward the fireplace, then dropped to one knee. "It's getting a little chilly, so I'll take care of the hearth."

"Sounds *gut.* I won't be long."

"Take your time."

After stopping in her bedroom to gather her nightclothes, Lavinia headed into the bathroom.

With her three active *youngies*, having a moment to herself was a luxury. Washing up, she dressed for bed.

Using the small mirror above the vanity as a guide, she unpinned her hair. Her tresses were long, hanging almost to the center of her back. The *Ordnung* didn't allow women to wear their hair down in public. Only when they were at home and in private were they allowed to remove their head coverings. Hair undone, she slathered raw coconut oil on her face. Though Amish women didn't wear cosmetics or other artificial enhancers, the use of natural or organic products was encouraged, particularly if it offered a health or medicinal benefit. She also used it as a conditioner on her hair and as an anti-inflammatory on cuts and scrapes.

Humming a breathless tune, she reflected on the busy week. Not only had she married and moved, but she'd also worked her fingers to the bone. Thanks to hard work, the old house had been turned into a habitable home. However, she wasn't exactly sure where she fit. Nothing was the way she'd expected it to be.

A sigh filtered through her lips. Her frustrations earlier in the day continued to linger in the back of her mind. Having been together such a brief time, she and Noem were still figuring each other out. They were friends, but they also weren't. They were man and wife, but they also weren't. Noem had done his best to make her feel welcome, but she didn't feel like a newlywed. She felt like a servant.

And then there was Josiah...

Despite his betrayal, she couldn't erase her first *ehmann* from her heart and insert Noem. Love and attraction were funny things, needing a spark to ignite. She didn't have those kinds of feelings toward the man she'd wed. Not yet.

Someday, maybe.

Put together for the evening, she paused to peek into the nursery. Penelope and Sophie were sleeping soundly. Jesse, too, had fallen into a doze. Save for the sound of a battery-powered fan to circulate the air, the nursery was peaceful.

Satisfied all was well, she walked down the short hall to the living room.

Bible in hand, Noem sat on the sofa. As promised, a cheery fire crackled in the fireplace. He glanced up, a smile parting his lips. "My, you look pretty. I didn't know your hair was so long."

Lavinia felt her cheeks warm with embarrassment. Though her modest sleeping attire covered almost every inch of her, it was the first time Noem had seen her out of her daily clothing. Thanks to the short hall, the back rooms of the house were out of direct view of the main living space. She could travel between the two bedrooms and the bathroom with an acceptable degree of privacy.

"Danke," she said, dropping her gaze. Usually, she braided her hair before she went to sleep, but tonight she'd let it hang free. Soft ebony curls fell in a cascade around her shoulders.

"I m-mean it." Glancing down at the pages, he quoted, "'Behold, thou art fair.'"

Lavinia's blush deepened. The quote was a familiar one during courtship, a poem in the Bible frequently recited as a relationship blossomed.

"Such sweet words are flattering." A laugh slipped past her lips. "But I am hardly fair of face. My eyes are set too far apart, my nose has too many freckles and my chin is too sharp."

After closing his Bible, Noem laid it aside. He stood and bridged the distance between them. "You are beautiful to me." Reaching out, he took her hands, cradling her smaller ones between his. "You always have been."

Heart skipping a beat, Lavinia felt drawn in by his expressive gaze and gentle touch. Save for the day they'd wed, they'd never stood in such close proximity to each other. They'd kept their distance, each mindful of the other's space. Almost twice her size, his frame dwarfed hers.

"You are too kind," she murmured, basking in the admiration reflected in his eyes. "But *Gott* warns us not to look on appearance with admiration."

"I'm only s-speaking the truth."

Lavinia cocked her head. Noem only stuttered when he was nervous or upset. His voice, too, had taken on a deeper timbre.

"Are you?"

Mouth twisting wryly, he blurted, "I wish I'd spoken up years ago—before you married Josiah."

Lavinia felt a curious tremble move through her. She wasn't sure if she should be dismayed or delighted.

Does he truly have feelings for me?

Or was Noem trying to convince himself he did now that they were bound in wedlock for the remainder of their lives?

Her fingers closed on his. "Why didn't you?"

Noem's face flushed a little. "Back then, I couldn't find the words," he confessed. "But I'm t-trying to now." His grip tightened subtly. "I know you don't love me, but I'd like a chance to change your mind."

Barely daring to breathe, Noem anxiously searched Lavinia's face. Disappointingly, she hadn't smiled. Instead, uncertainty rippled through her expression. Though she didn't pull away from his hold, neither did she give any reply.

Feeling foolish, he wished he'd kept his emotions to himself. Had he offended her in some way? He wasn't sure. "I'm s-sorry," he stammered. "I didn't mean any offense." Releasing her hands, he stepped away.

Breathless, lips half parted, Lavinia gazed at him through dewy eyes. "I'm touched you have feelings for me," she said, breaking her long silence. "I can honestly say I have always liked you, too."

Her reply was music to his ears. Given a reprieve from his embarrassment, he felt relief filter through him. "I'm glad to hear you say that."

"As for whether my feelings will ever turn to more…" As she held up a hand, a light blush colored her pale cheeks. "Truly, I don't think I know what love is. Looking back, I realize I made mistakes letting my heart rule my head when I was still a girl. Now that I am older, you'll have to forgive me for being more, um, careful to guard my emotions."

"I know I'm not the m-man you imagined you'd spend your life with," Noem said, fighting to master his recalcitrant tongue. "But I'm your humble servant in every way. I always will be."

The edges of her eyes moistened, rimming with tears. "It's not you, Noem. It's other things—" As if ripped from the very depths of her being, a sigh sifted through her lips. "Would it sound cruel if I said I'd sometimes like to be able to rearrange the past?"

"I'm not sure what you mean."

Regret shadowed her face. "Just tear a few pages out of the book of my life?"

His brows rose in surprise. "I suppose there are times when we all want to pluck a page or two out."

"I would," she said softly. "I'd tear out the pages of my marriage to Josiah and throw them away." Gaze flitting away, some deep inner distress ridged her jaw. "If I could."

Noem gazed into her conflicted face. "He hurt you very badly, didn't he?"

A frown turned down the corners of her mouth. Lowering her head, she allowed a tiny nod. *"Ja,"* she murmured in a voice barely heard. "He did."

Shock filled him. He'd had no idea how badly she might have suffered. "Did he physically strike you or Sophie?"

"Nein. He never lifted a hand against us." Again, silence followed.

"But?"

Discontent and agony simmered beneath the surface of her calm. "Josiah was a liar." A tear escaped her control, then another. Shaking overwhelmed her fragile composure. She quickly brushed the tears away, refusing to give in to her inner anguish. "The Lord warns that men use their tongues to deceive. But for my own *ehmann* to do it… It was more than I could bear."

"Then he wasn't an honest man?"

"*Nein.* He was neither honest nor trustworthy. Josiah chose to live in deception, cloaking himself in untruths." Pausing, she shook her head. "I say I have forgiven him, but my words often ring hollow to my ears. I have struggled to let the past go, but it keeps rising back up to haunt me."

"I'm sorry," he said softly. "I had no idea he'd hurt you so badly."

Stepping back, Lavinia kept her robe tucked close to her body. "I confess that I've been disobedient to *Gott* for my inability to truly forgive Josiah," she said, moving around him to take a seat on the sofa. Sitting, she continued in a weary tone, "How can I expect the Lord to bless my future if I can't let go of my past?"

"You're human," he countered. "We all are. You're being too hard on yourself."

She looked at him through hopeful eyes. "You think so?"

"I do."

"You're a better man than I deserve," she said, shaking her head in disbelief. "And you deserve an *ehefrau* who adores you with all her heart. I wish I could give you that now, but I can't. That fault lies with me. It's time for me to move on. I want to…"

"But you can't." Not a question.

"Ecclesiastes warns us it's better not to make a vow we can't keep." Sadness again shadowed her tired, strained face. "So, please, don't ask me if I can ever love you back. I can't give you an answer. Not now. Maybe not ever." Her voice trembled with pain and regret, and a heartbreaking smile sealed her words.

Shaken and distressed by her confession, Noem swallowed the lump building in his throat. Though he and Josiah had never been friends, he had nothing against the man and believed him to be a decent fellow. But if he were to believe Lavinia's words—and he did— then the face Josiah presented to the public was a mask that hid a deeply flawed human being.

It is for Gott *to judge Josiah.*

As for Lavinia… He was impressed by the way she carried herself. Acting with quiet dignity and discretion, she'd kept her woes private. She was not a woman given to complaints and went about her business with her head held high and her lips sealed shut. If she cried or gnashed her teeth in frustration, she did so out of his sight. Her discreet composure only made him admire her more.

"Forgive me for adding more weight to your burden." Ashamed he'd let desire overcome his sense, Noem let his hands hang limply at his sides. He ached to hold her close, to soothe away her pain, but doubted she would welcome his embrace. "I shan't ask for anything but your prayers. And for you, my dearest, I will pray *Gott* ministers to you through Ezekiel," he said, and then quoted, "'A new heart also will I give you, and a new spirit will I put within you.'"

Lavinia's eyes flooded with fresh tears. "Oh, Noem... You have given me mercy and shelter in my time of darkness." Pain flickered through her expression. A light tremble moved her slight frame. "I—oh—" Her voice cracked, forlorn and wretched with emotion.

Knots of frustration tightened his stomach. "I know you don't feel anything for me now. But since we're married for the rest of our lives, I've got plenty of time to fix what Josiah broke. All I'm asking for is a chance."

She dabbed at her eyes. "You dear, sweet

man…" she murmured, forcing a smile through her sadness.

A sudden wail from the nursery shattered the silence filling the house.

Summoned by the demanding need of the *boppli*, Lavinia jumped to her feet. "Sounds like someone is unhappy." Rushing away, she disappeared down the hall. A few minutes passed before she returned, cradling his unhappy nephew. "I'd hoped the medicine would allow him to get some sleep."

Noem eyed the fretful infant. "Doesn't look like anyone will get much tonight."

Lavinia nodded toward the kitchen. "Would you get one of his teething rings out of the icebox? I put a few inside to chill. That will help soothe his sore mouth."

"On it." Hurrying to complete the task, Noem handed the item over.

Settling in her rocking chair, Lavinia offered the infant the teether. "There you go, little one."

Distressed, Jesse grunted and batted the ring away. "Maah!"

She tried again, holding the little *boi* in an upright position. "Bite."

Jesse stubbornly refused. Something else had caught his attention, and he was determined to have it. Extending grasping hands, he grabbed her cascading curls. "Ah!" he cried, pulling them toward his mouth.

"*Ach*, no!" Lavinia exclaimed, struggling to free her locks. "He's never seen me with my hair down. I usually braid it and tuck it under my bed cap after a bath."

"Let me." Bending, Noem gently pried open tiny fingers, releasing the strands.

"Better?"

"Much. *Danke* for helping." Lavinia offered the teething ring again. Jesse grabbed it and shoved it into his mouth. He gnawed with enthusiasm, content to be held.

Entranced by the length and softness of her tresses, Noem swept aside a stray lock caressing her cheek. "May I put up your hair?"

Giving him a look, Lavinia started to shake her head. Pausing halfway through, she nodded instead. "*Ja*. You may. My hairbrush and ties are on the vanity in the washroom."

"I'll get them." Pleased she'd agreed, Noem hurried to grab the items. Finding what he needed, he returned to stand behind her chair.

Slowly taking in a handful, he began at the snarled tips. Her long hair, black as a raven's wing, was truly her glory. Drawing the brush through the thick strands, he savored the fragrant scent of the coconut oil she used as a conditioner.

"Is this okay? I'm not hurting you?"

Sighing, Lavinia closed her eyes. "*Ach*, no. I love having my hair brushed. It's so relaxing."

Pleased she'd allowed him the liberty, Noem drew upon a deep well of gentle patience. When she was ready for a relationship, she would let him know. Until then, he could only wait—and pray—his *ehefrau* would, someday, come to love him.

"I know I haven't said it, but I appreciate all you've brought into our lives," he murmured, again pulling the stiff bristles in a downward arc. "I know everything seemed like a disaster from the beginning. You haven't had a break the entire week."

"It's not your fault. Callie's passing put you in a hard place. I understand you didn't have much time to pull things together. And you have done everything you promised. I have no complaint."

Once he'd laid the brush aside, Noem took her hair in handfuls and separated it for braiding. "But it's so crowded here. I know the lack of space is frustrating." Giving her thick tresses a light tug, he passed one strand over the other to create a single long rope of hair. "You'll have better. A big house, with plenty of rooms. I promise. It'll take a year or so to build a new one, so I plan to start looking at properties for sale. You wouldn't mind living in town?"

"Why, no. I don't suppose I would."

Finished, Noem secured her hair with a band. "There's a couple of properties I've passed by on my way to work that have for-sale signs. I might stop and look." Remembering his *daed*'s advice, he added, "Perhaps we could go together."

She nodded. "It would be nice to get out and ride around."

Done with his task, Noem returned her brush to the washroom, careful to put it back where he'd found it.

"It's a date," he said, coming back into the living room. "We'll find some time this week and get out on our own. Perhaps we could ask Mrs. Graff to come over and help *Daed* watch the *youngies*. Then it would just be you and me for a few hours."

Lavinia smiled up at him. "I would like that."

Tired of his teething ring, Jesse began to doze. Passing midnight, the hours had begun to circle toward the new day.

"I think I'll try putting him down again." Standing, she pressed the sleepy *boppli* to her shoulder, patting him lightly on the back. "*Danke* for staying up." As she tilted back her head, warmth lit her gaze. "We've both had a rough time. Before I go to sleep, I will pray the Lord grants us calm waters through our journey together."

Encouraged, Noem put out a hand and gently touched her cheek. "May I—" the words stumbled across his tongue, but he forced himself to finish "—kiss you goodnight?"

Dark lashes brushed rosy cheeks. *"Ja."*

Barely daring to breathe, Noem stepped closer and cupped her face. Lowering his head, he brushed his mouth over hers.

Need had brought them together.

But it was hope that would usher them into tomorrow.

Chapter Ten

Noem couldn't recall a time when he'd ever been reluctant to get up and go to work. He'd spent nearly a decade at the buggy shop and enjoyed the challenges his job presented. Most days there weren't enough hours to complete all his projects. He often bunked down at the shop just to save himself the trouble of going home at night.

Through a whirlwind of days, everything changed in his life. Not only had he taken custody of his niece and nephew, but he'd also gotten married. His life was no longer his own. A wife and three *youngies* demanded his attention now, taking up every minute of his day.

And it was wonderful.

His drab life had burst into a kaleidoscope of color and sound. There was always something that needed to be taken care of: a repair to be made, a *kind* to be changed, a mess to be cleaned up. Chasing after the *kinder*, he'd never been more engaged. Watching the little ones grow and explore their new world opened his eyes. The responsibility was exciting and frightening. Without exactly knowing when, he'd become a *familie* man. And a man took care of his responsibilities. If it meant working an hour longer and harder, he'd do it. They depended on him as the head of the household to provide a strong role model, guiding all with a firm but loving hand. He'd also made a promise that Callie's memory would live on through Penelope and Jesse. When they were older, both he and Lavinia had many stories to share about their *mamm*. Despite the mistakes she'd made, neither felt Callie's memory should be erased from her *kinder*'s lives. Callie would always have a place in their home. Her tragedy had brought them all together. She'd mended their tattered lives, binding them to each other. Her one life had touched many others, and she wouldn't be forgotten.

Letting the reins dangle in his hands, Noem lounged back on the hard wooden seat. With so many things buzzing through his head, it was hard to keep his focus on the road. He hadn't slept a wink preferring to replay the wonderful hour he'd spent with Lavinia. Letting the images unspool through his mind, he savored the moments. He could still recall the enticing scent of her hair as he'd pulled the brush through her long tresses. They'd shared a kiss, too. The softness of her warm lips was still imprinted on his.

After drawing in a breath, Noem released a sigh. He'd never envisioned himself being married to one of the prettiest girls in Humble. The joy of those precious memories filled him with happiness. He ached to embrace his *ehefrau* and cover her beautiful face with kisses. To win her heart—and her trust—he'd have to prove he was a man worth having.

Rejoice in hope and be patient in tribulation.

The sudden honk of a truck's horn shoved him out of his thoughts.

Lips pressing flat, Noem tightened his grip on the reins guiding his horse as a massive delivery truck sped past his buggy. Blasting the horn, the driver swerved dangerously close on the narrow two-lane strip.

Frightened by the assault, his startled mare whinnied, shifting from a slow walk to a spirited run.

Stomach twisting, Noem's heart thudded against his rib cage. The clip-clopping of iron horseshoes striking asphalt echoed in his ears.

Close to panic, he forced himself to tamp down his fright. Lose control and the horse could veer off the road, galloping into a ditch.

Fearful of an overturned carriage, he pulled back on the reins. "Bessie, mind yourself!" Thankfully, the horse slowed, resuming a normal pace.

Englisch drivers were so careless. Instead of heeding the safety of slower-moving vehicles, drivers often roared by without thinking.

Englisch hurry for nothing.

Relieved he'd avoided a terrible accident, Noem pushed his hat back, wiping the perspiration off his brow. His heart had yet to slow back into a normal rhythm.

He drew in a breath to steady himself. A snippet of Proverbs came into his mind. *"Be not afraid of sudden fear...for the Lord shall be thy confidence."*

Noem tipped his head heavenward. *"Danke* for keeping a hand over me, *Gott."*

Setting his eyes firmly on the road ahead, he gave Bessie's behind a flick to hurry her trot. Traffic thickened as he approached the outskirts of Humble, a mix of gas-powered vehicles and other Amish folks. Though Humble wasn't a large town, it was a busy one.

Merging into traffic, he headed toward Zeb Yoder's shop. Normally the trip into town took less than thirty minutes. He was late because he'd allowed himself to dally and daydream. By the time he turned onto the path that would take him to the employee parking barn, he was more than half an hour behind.

He hopped out of his buggy and left it in the care of the attendant who looked after the horses through the long workday. The animals needed to be fed, walked and watered. As Zeb only hired Amish folks, he'd had the presence of mind to provide amenities that would accommodate their unique needs. Other employers hired vans to pick up their Amish workers, transporting them to and from work. And those who hadn't yet made a commitment to the church were allowed to drive. A lot of Amish teens acquired cars and other means of transportation during their *rumspringa* and were more than happy to offer a ride.

Having left the barn, Noem hurried through the side door of the warehouse. The building was huge, an assembly line of equipment geared toward the mass production of buggies. Although hand planes, saws, hammers and chisels were commonplace, the workers also had pneumatic tools. Instead of electricity, those tools ran on an air compressor fueled by a diesel engine. Solar panels powered the lights and other small devices needed to keep the shop running at full capacity.

His coworkers greeted him as he entered the employee break room. Like himself, they wore similar clothes: black broadfall trousers, plain white shirts and heavy black boots. Black suspenders finished their simple outfits.

"*Gut* to see you back, Noem," Rohm Stoltz greeted.

"*Gut* to be back," he returned, nodding at the ruddy-faced older man.

"I was sorry to hear about Callie's passing," Rohm continued, laying a hand on his shoulder in sympathy. "May she rest in peace."

"*Danke.*"

"It was *gut* of you to take her *youngies*." A question mark shadowed his features. "But didn't she have an *Englisch ehmann*?"

"Erik left her a while back," he replied, deciding the truth was the best way to explain things. "There was no one else to take her *kinder.*"

Rohm shook his head. "*Ach*, a shame that is."

"I almost fell out of my seat when Bishop Graber announced you'd be marrying Josiah Simmons's widow," Peter Ableson added.

"Didn't think you'd be the marrying kind," Rohm said.

Noem licked papery lips. He'd known there

would be questions when he came back to work. Callie's unexpected passing followed by his sudden marriage had surprised a lot of people. "Bishop Graber suggested it would be beneficial for me and Lavinia to join our households." He kept his explanation simple. Gossip would go around no matter what he had to say.

"My *tante* Ella had a companion marriage," Peter volunteered. "They had a *gut* twenty years together before her second *ehmann* passed."

Noem gave his friend a curious look. "What happened after that?"

Peter grimaced wryly. "Why, she went on to marry two more times."

Relaxing a bit, Noem offered a smile. "I can honestly say I'm planning for this to be my first and last marriage."

Conversation falling to a lull, the men walked toward their workstations. Though the hour was an early one, the shop hummed with activity. Set up like an assembly line, men worked with precise and efficient movements. The roar of pneumatically driven power tools drowned out almost every other sound. Buggies in all stages of assembly filled the warehouse. Most had been custom ordered and would be outfitted to the buyer's precise specifications. Each vehicle would be crafted with care and took several months to produce.

Glad to be back, Noem headed toward the buggy he'd been customizing. The buyer had asked for running lights, among other "modern" conveniences. Everything would be battery-powered and operated by a series of switches on a custom-crafted dash. Running behind, he'd have to put in a few late nights to meet the promised deadline.

He was about to begin working on the wiring when Zeb Yoder ambled over. An older man with a deeply wrinkled face and tufts of white hair sneaking out from under his hat, he'd owned the shop for sixty years.

"I heard you were back," he said as a greeting.

Noem straightened. "*Ja. Danke* for giving me the time off. I appreciate it."

Zeb's expression was veiled with compassion. "You had *familie* things to look after. 'Twas a sad thing, Callie passing so suddenly. You have my sympathy."

"I appreciate that."

"I have to admit it raised a few brows that you married Lavinia Simmons," Zeb continued. "Always thought you'd be an old bachelor."

"I believed so myself, but *Gott* changed my path."

"Glad things worked out."

"I'm thankful the Lord's lent a hand."

"Lot of changes for a man to go through all at once. Almost hate to be putting more on you now."

"More?" Noem parroted. "I don't understand."

Zeb crossed his arms. "You know I've been meaning to sell the shop. And I know you'd planned to make an offer."

Insides clenching, Noem offered a nod. A man who'd only produced daughters, Zeb had no *sohns* to pass his business to. The men his girls had married had trades of their own.

"*Ja.* I've been saving my wages since I started."

Eyeing Noem's worn work clothes, Zeb laughed. "I figured you had. I've never known a thriftier man, except maybe your *daed.* Don't think a penny's ever gotten away from him."

Noem grinned. "I think he pinches them until they cry." It was no secret both his parents were notoriously tightfisted. He wasn't sure how much money his *daed* had tucked away, but he figured it was a considerable amount.

"Well, there's no beating around the bush. I'm selling. You'd be the first I'd consider."

Noem's guts knotted tighter, causing a faint

rise of nausea. He'd known the day would arrive soon. He'd intended to have cash in hand when Zeb decided the time was right.

Except now he wasn't so excited.

Sick at heart, he swallowed back disappointment. He'd promised Lavinia a bigger house for their growing *familie*.

And therein lay the problem.

He had the money for one or the other. But he didn't have the funds to cover both.

Gazing across the table, Lavinia eyed her *ehmann*. Over the last few days, something in Noem had changed. Forehead deeply ridged, a frown replaced his usual smile. Hardly making eye contact when he spoke, he'd descended into silence. Shadows haunted his expression. He barely ate, picking at his food with little enthusiasm.

Stomach knotting, she set her fork aside. Her appetite had vanished. She couldn't figure out what she'd done to put him in a bad mood. After the lovely time they'd spent together following Sunday's Easter activities, she'd believed they'd come to an understanding. But within a few days, everything had crumbled, taking them back to square one. Noem had shut down. He spoke only when spoken to, and his replies were clipped.

He's not happy.

And neither was she.

Living under the tension wasn't only shredding her nerves, it was affecting the *youngies*. The relationship they'd begun to build had fallen apart, slipping through her fingers. She'd believed him when he'd told her he wanted them to work toward having a real marriage. Now she wasn't so sure. She'd already been tied to a man whose word she couldn't count on. What if Noem did the same—saying one thing to her face, yet doing as he pleased behind her back?

Despair twisted her insides. Tears misted her eyes, blurring her vision. *I can't live like this.*

Sitting between them, Gabriel looked from one to the other. "*Ach*, I've never seen such miserable faces. You two have barely spoken in days."

Releasing a sigh, Noem refused to make eye contact. "I've got a lot on my mind. I just don't feel like talking."

"Like what?"

Noem pushed his food around on his plate. "Work stuff."

The old man squinted. "Work stuff has nothin' to do with home stuff."

"What do you mean?"

"You're a newly married man, so you're still

figurin' things out." A wry chuckle escaped. "First thing you gotta learn is when you're at work, those problems belong there. Leave them at the door when you come home. Ain't no cause to burden your *ehefrau* and *kinder* with things they ain't got no control over."

Noem's brow ridged. "I hadn't thought about it that way." His voice took on a gentler tone. "I was so caught up in my problems, I didn't stop to think how it affected everyone else."

"A man's always gonna have problems. One of the first things I learned after I married your *mamm* was to cast my anxieties to the Lord at the end of the day. Somehow, things I'd worried about weren't so bad when I let them sit overnight," Gabriel said.

"I should have known to do that." Sitting up, Noem straightened his shoulders. "Forgive me for acting like a fool."

Gabriel sniffed. "I'm not the one you owe an apology to."

Listening to the exchange, Lavinia felt relief wash through her. She hadn't expected her father-in-law to take her side in the matter. But the older man had delivered a lesson from the Lord with candor and wisdom. Given how unwelcoming Gabriel was at the beginning of their marriage, she marveled at the changes in his manner. All it took was one little *bop-*

pli grabbing his beard to crack the sorrow encasing his heart. Reserve crumbling, Gabriel had embraced his *enkelkinder* with open arms. He'd even welcomed Sophie, treating her like his own.

Chastened, Noem found her gaze. "Lavinia, I'm sorry for the way I've been acting. I had a few things on my mind, and I let worry get the best of me."

She picked up the napkin she'd spread across her lap and dabbed at her eyes. "I believed I'd done something to displease you."

"Not at all. It wasn't you or the *youngies*." Pausing, he blew out a frustrated breath. "Some things happened at work. I've been racking my brain trying to figure out what to do."

Folding her napkin, she placed it neatly beside her plate. Most of her food was untouched. "Anything you care to share, I will listen. Even if I'm only a *frau* and have no *gut* advice, I will be there for you. Always."

"I've been trying to figure out a way to tell you, but I didn't know how."

"Oh?"

"Ja." Noem pushed his chair back, rose and carried his plate to the sink. Placing his hands against the edges of the counter, he lowered his head. His shoulders sagged.

"A man doesn't hide things from his *ehe-frau, sohn*," Gabriel prodded.

Noem turned. "You're right."

Gabriel gave Penelope and Sophie a look. Sensing the tension between the adults, they sat quietly at their little table. "Tiny ears don't need to hear what grown-ups have to say." He nodded toward the front door. "Your *mamm* and I used to sit in the porch swing and do our talkin'."

Noem turned. "That's a *gut* idea."

Nerves clenching, Lavinia offered a nod. She had no idea what had happened, but she supposed she'd find out soon enough.

"Give me a minute to see after the *young-gies*." Rising, she lifted Jesse from his high-chair. Face and hands coated with the oatmeal he'd had for supper, he'd amused everyone with his attempts to feed himself. He'd dipped his hands into the bowl and smeared the cereal all over his face and body.

"Gak!" he squealed.

Kissing his messy face, she couldn't help smiling. "Someone needs a bath."

Gabriel reached for the *boppli*. "I'll look after him. Take a moment to yourselves. I can keep an eye on the *youngies*."

Lavinia handed the squirming *boi* over. *"Danke."* Smoothing her apron with nervous hands, she followed Noem outside. She'd recently begun to tend Amelia's flower boxes, cleaning them out in preparation to plant an array of colorful flowers.

Noem sat. "Well, here we are."

"Ja." Settling beside him, Lavinia folded her hands in her lap. The day was beginning to fade as the sun dropped toward the horizon, stealing warmth and light. Shadows darkened the trees shading the property. "Here we are."

Leaning forward, Noem placed his elbows on his knees. Keeping his head down, he stared at his boots. "I guess I might as well just come out and say what I've got to say."

"Please—go ahead."

"I guess you don't know, but Zeb Yoder's been planning to retire."

"Ja. I'd heard that around town."

"Before all this happened with Callie, I'd been planning to put in a bid to buy his business. It's a *gut* living. Instead of being an employee, I'd be boss."

"Then why are you worried?" Relieved, her concern flitted away. "It sounds like a wonderful opportunity."

Noem sat up, turning to face her. "When we got married, I promised you a bigger house." His expression tensed. "But if I buy Zeb out, I can't afford it."

Surprised by his confession, she huffed in disbelief. "And you think I'll be disappointed if I don't get a new house?"

Shamefaced, he offered a nod. *"Ja."* Swallowing hard, he added, "I'm going to tell Zeb I can't."

Lavinia immediately waved her hands, indicating the opposite. *"Nein.* You are to tell Zeb you will buy the business."

"B-but—"

"This is your living we are talking about. A house can be gotten any time. You'd be foolish to let such an opportunity pass."

"If I do, it'll wipe out my savings. It'd be a few years before I could afford to get us something of our own."

"If Zeb is giving you a fair deal, you should take it."

His expression lightened. "You wouldn't be mad having to wait?"

She offered a reassuring squeeze. "There's nothing wrong with this house. No doubt, it's small. But it's home."

"I was worried you would be angry I'd deceived you into marrying me."

"On the contrary. I'm proud you want to do better. And I know the Lord will bless your diligence."

As if tossed a lifeline, all the tension drained

from his expression. "I apologize for being out of sorts. It seemed like my life fell apart when Callie passed. But I was wrong. Even though I couldn't imagine how, everything is working out."

"Oh, ye of little faith." She laughed. "That's the power of *Gott*. Whatever burden you carry, the Lord will help you bear it." Pausing, she met his gaze. "So will I… If you'll let me."

"Really?"

"Of course, silly. You've worked your whole life for this."

"It's not just for me—" he started to say.

"I know. It's for us. For *our* future." Without thinking, she reached up and touched his cheek. "I'm so proud of my *ehmann*."

As if casting off a millstone, his shoulders straightened. "Then it's settled. I'll go to the bank and have a check drawn up for Zeb tomorrow." Gripping her hands, a smile brightened his face. "I'm so blessed I married a woman who led me back to living the way the Lord intended." Lifting her hands to his lips, he pressed a kiss against her fingertips.

Surprised, Lavinia gasped as warmth swirled down her spine. Her pulse fluttered, doubling its beat. Longing gripped her heart.

"I am blessed you asked."

Encouraged, Noem leaned closer. His lips were barely an inch from hers.

Closing her eyes, Lavinia tipped her head. Her senses sharpened with anticipation.

But nothing happened.

The crunch of tires on gravel interrupted. After pulling into the drive, a long-haired man dressed in jeans and a T-shirt exited a beat-up pickup. His massive biceps were covered with crude tattoos. A heavy mustache and beard blurred half his face.

Startled, Noem jumped to his feet. "Now, who could that be?" He crossed the deck, looking through the screen door. "We're not expecting company."

Catching sight of the visitor, Lavinia stiffened. A shiver tore up her spine. *He looks like trouble.*

"I'll go have a word," Noem said.

Lavinia also stood. Her legs wobbled beneath her weight. "Be careful."

Noem opened the screen door. "I will." He trotted down the steps, and then strode across the yard and into the driveway. "Can I help you?"

The stranger slammed the driver-side door. "I'm looking for Josiah Simmons's wife."

Lavinia felt her blood pressure drop. An arctic rush of ice filled her veins. Her guess was correct. Another gambler holding one of Josiah's IOUs had come to collect.

"Be careful, Noem," she murmured, watching from behind. Gott, *protect him.*

Noem answered the stranger with a nod. "*Ja.* Except her name isn't Simmons. It's Witzel, and she's married to me." He crossed his arms. "Anything you have to say to her, you can say to me."

"I'm here to collect my money. Josiah owed me a grand. That's a thousand dollars, and I intend to have it. Today."

"Maybe you haven't heard, but Josiah's passed."

"Yeah, I heard. But I was in jail and couldn't pay my respects," the man snarled back. "Now that I'm out, I could use the money." A snort followed. "That Plain boy had no luck about him."

Noem stood his ground. "I don't know what Josiah's vices were. And I don't care. The way I figure it is any debt he had died with him."

Spitting out a wad of chewing tobacco, the stranger hitched his thumbs in the pockets of his jeans and rocked back on his heels. "The way I figure it is if Josiah can't pay, then his wife can."

"You won't get a dime from my wife or me," Noem countered, shaking his head. "You need to leave. Now."

"I'm thinking different." Stepping forward, the intruder gave Noem a hard shove.

Caught off guard by the violence, Noem lifted his hands. "Hey, there's no reason to get mad."

Releasing a scornful laugh, the stranger advanced. "I'm not mad." An ugly chuckle slipped past his lips. "I'm just giving you a little persuasion to pay up."

Chapter Eleven

Heart leaping to her throat, Lavinia felt a wild cry rip past her lips. "Stop, please!" She clenched her fists against a flood of dread. The confrontation between the two men had turned violent. Rooted in place, her feet felt like lead weights.

Gabriel rushed onto the veranda. "What's goin' on? I heard yellin'."

Gathering her wits, Lavinia glanced at his empty arms. Through the open door behind him, she saw that he'd set Jesse down in his playpen. Upset over his abandonment, the *boppli* squalled at the top of his lungs. Penelope and Sophie hovered near the door. Faces pale and eyes wide as saucers, the girls whimpered with fear and confusion.

Swooping to gather them up, she lifted both into her arms. Their tear-stained faces pressed against her neck even as their arms gripped her for dear life.

Breath coming in ragged gasps, she hurried to explain. "A man is looking for me. Josiah owed him money. He wants Noem to pay him."

Even as she tried to shield the *youngies*, the terrible scene continued to play out. She didn't want to look again, but fear for Noem's safety yanked her gaze back to the fight. Heart slamming against her ribcage, she sent up a prayer.

Oh, Lord, please lay your hand over him.

Noem wasn't a fighter. Physical violence among the Amish was rare. They preferred to handle disagreements civilly.

The scuffle between the two men continued. Snarling words she couldn't make out, the scruffy *Englischer* cocked his arm and launched his fist forward with brute force.

Ducking to dodge the blow, Noem stumbled back. His clumsy move wasn't fast enough. The man's fist connected with his jaw. Stunned by the unprovoked attack, Noem dropped to the ground.

The stranger towered over him. "I want what Josiah owes me," he growled and kicked out.

Noem attempted to roll out of the way, but the stranger's boot caught him on the temple.

"Give me my money!" Hands clenching

open and shut, the stranger delivered a second blow.

Dragging himself to his feet, Noem refused to back down. "You'll get nothing here," he warned and grabbed a hoe lying nearby. He brandished the garden implement like a sword. With two prongs on one side and a sharp blade on the other, it could do a lot of damage. "The Lord says we are to turn the other cheek when struck, but this isn't one of those times." Mouth a grim line, he stood ready to defend himself.

The scruffy man sneered: "You want to fight, Amish?" Reaching into his back pocket, he fished out a metal object with four circular holes. He slid his fingers through it, and four short prongs protruded from his knuckles. A sneer twisted his lips. "Let's do it."

Though events seemed to move in slow motion, only a few seconds had passed. The two men's movements were a blur of action and reaction.

Seeing the danger, Gabriel didn't hesitate. Intent on helping his *sohn*, he pushed through the screen door and rushed down the steps. He stopped long enough to pick up the shovel lying near one of the flower beds.

"Leave him be!" As if to make sure the stranger knew he was serious, Gabriel advanced. He cocked the shovel above his shoulder, ready to swing. "I ain't foolin' around."

Outnumbered, the stranger raised his hands. Suddenly, he wasn't so brave or bold.

"Two against one ain't fair."

Hoe in hand, Noem took a step forward. "You just get on out of here and don't come back."

The man backed toward his vehicle and opened the door. Sliding behind the wheel, he twisted the ignition. Lacking a muffler and belching black smoke, the old pickup roared to life. Slamming into Reverse, he hit the accelerator, scattering gravel in all directions. In a last act of defiance, he waved a clenched fist. Peeling out, his truck disappeared down the drive.

Staggering a little, Noem dropped the hoe. "Looks like we scared him off."

After tossing the shovel aside, Gabriel rushed to Noem's side and offered a steadying hand. "I'm here for you, *sohn*. Lean on me." Turning Noem around, he led him toward the house.

With his palm pressed against his temple, Noem's mouth was a flat line. "Can't believe I let him hit me."

Lavinia's gaze raked over her *ehmann* as he walked up the steps. When he reached the porch, Noem collapsed onto the swing. Blood stained his hand, oozing through his fingers. Dark bruises circled his eyes.

"You're hurt." Her quavering voice faltered and failed. Sensing her anxiety, Penelope and Sophie both burst into tears. Unarmed and unused to fighting, Noem had done his best to keep the peace.

"We need to get you to the hospital," Gabriel urged. "I'll get the buggy."

Noem sucked in a breath. *"Nein."* As though trying to prove he was all right, he sat up straighter. His hand fell away from his temple. "I'm not hurt that bad."

Unable to stand the sight of his injuries, Lavinia clenched her eyes shut. With two babes in her arms and another bawling in his playpen, helplessness swept through her. Her heart thudded harder, threatening to pound its way through her ribs. She'd never been so terrified. Fear pulsed through her veins as hundreds of horrible scenarios tumbled through her mind. What if the man was armed with a gun? What if Gabriel hadn't been able to help? What would have happened if the stranger had arrived when she was home alone with the *youngies*? Each question frightened her more than the one before.

The crunch of horses' hooves on the gravel

drive jarred her out of her fear. Buggy rolling to a stop, a familiar figure jumped down. Abram dashed through the gate and hurried up the porch steps.

"What are you doing here?"

Face shadowed with concern, Abram's gaze swept over Noem. "I was afraid this would happen. Looks like I'm too late." Before anyone could speak, he added, "The *Englisch* folks who bought your house let us know a man came around asking for Josiah. Unfortunately, they told him Lavinia had remarried and where to find her. I thought I'd better come and give you a warning." He eyed Noem's injured face. "Guess I wasn't fast enough."

Gabriel nodded emphatically. "Noem took a few licks but held his own."

Visually searching Noem's injuries, Abram's eyes narrowed. "You sure you're okay?"

Noem offered a nod. "*Ja*. I'm fine. I tried being sensible, but he wasn't willing to listen. But don't think I didn't defend myself. Even though I hated raising a weapon against another man, I think that fella got the message Plain folks aren't helpless."

"I'm not for hurtin' anyone," Gabriel added. "But you can't turn the other cheek when a man's attackin' you and intendin' to do harm. Isn't that so, Minister?"

Abram nodded. "People have a right to protect themselves and their loved ones. There is no biblical command against reasonably defending ourselves." He eyed Noem again. "Maybe you ought to let a doctor look at that."

Waving a hand, Noem stood. "Just give me a minute to clear my head." He added, "Don't need to see no doctor."

"We should at least get the swelling down," Abram said. "That's going to leave a nasty bruise."

Heart returning to a normal beat, Lavinia found her voice. An icy wave of reason calmed her. "Someone help me with these *youngies* and I'll make a compress." Lowering Penelope and Sophie, she glanced through the open doorway. Dragging himself to one corner of his playpen, Jesse then managed to sit up. As he clung to the side, his face was red from bawling.

"I need you both to play quietly," she continued, ushering the girls inside. "Do you think you can do that?"

Penelope tugged her skirt. Though not yet five, she often displayed a sense of maturity beyond her years. A natural caregiver, she loved helping. "I can."

Sophie also tugged. "Me can."

Fetching their dolls, the girls went to play in the living room.

"Now we will be mamas and take care of our babies," Penelope instructed.

The men followed. As Abram headed for the crib, Noem and Gabriel went into the kitchen.

Bending over, Abram lifted Jesse to his shoulder, and patted the *boppli*'s back. "There now. No need to cry."

"Gumph!" Settling down, Jesse crammed his hand into his mouth, gnawing at his fingers. Drool poured down his chin.

Noem snuffled a laugh. "That babe sounds about like I feel." Bending over the kitchen sink, he flipped on the tap and splashed water on his face. "Might feel better if I bawled a little, too."

Lavinia pointed to a chair. "Sit down so I can have a look at that."

"Yes, ma'am." Following instructions, Noem took a seat.

Slipping a hand under his chin, Lavinia angled his head toward the light. Noem had taken quite a blow to the temple. The scrape from the stranger's boot wasn't a deep one, but it had broken the skin and left an ugly bruise.

Having assessed the damage, she fetched a few pieces of ice. She wrapped them in a dish towel and pressed the makeshift compress against his wound. "Thank *Gott* you don't need stitches."

He offered a smile. *"Danke."*

"You should go to the police," Abram advised.

Noem spread his hands in dismay. "Everything happened so fast that I didn't even get his license plate number."

"Got it right here," Gabriel said and tapped his forehead.

"He's already gone. There isn't much they can do now."

Lavinia pursed her lips. Because the Amish were such a tight-knit group, local law enforcement usually preferred to let the members of the Plain community police themselves. However, there was a different outlook when an *Englischer* committed an offense. At such times, the bishop encouraged folks to cooperate with local officers.

"If this man's hurt you, he will hurt others," Abram said in a grave tone. "They might not be so lucky to walk away."

A wry grimace twisted Noem's face. "I suppose you're right."

"I'd like to file a complaint myself," Abram added. "I am not happy he's sniffing around. I don't want him coming on the *familie* property looking for Lavinia, either."

Gabriel looked straight at Abram. "I'd like

to know why the fella was comin' around demandin' money in the first place."

Lavinia froze. When she'd agreed to marry Noem, she'd hoped to put that part of her past behind her. But her deception had an unintended consequence.

The Lord says the truth will set us free. I can't carry Josiah's sin any longer.

Drawing back her shoulders, she placed her palm against her middle to steady her nerves. Her insides were full of painful knots. "Josiah was a gambler. He lost everything we had."

Eyes narrowing, Gabriel scratched his bearded chin. "People have been sayin' he was into some bad business."

"It's true. He couldn't stay away from the cards and the dice." Refusing to look away, Lavinia kept her gaze steady. "I'm ashamed to say it, but I only found out after he passed. I didn't know he'd mortgaged our property— or that he owed so much money."

The old man's brow darkened with thunderous anger. "I knew it wasn't any *gut* when they let that casino come in! We should have done more to stop it."

Abram stepped up. "I agree you're right to be angry. Unfortunately, it had the support of the city council. They wanted the jobs it would create, plus the benefit to other businesses. We have a lot of tourists come through. Once they're done shopping, they want to be entertained."

"Wasn't a *gut* thing letting *Englischers* move in. Their ways are against everything we believe," Gabriel argued. "And our youth are sufferin' the consequences."

"Leviticus commands that we love the strangers among us as we love ourselves," Abram countered with gentle wisdom. "All we can do is hold to our own beliefs and let *Gott* take care of the rest."

Reluctantly, Lavinia lifted her head. "I'm so ashamed. I didn't know Josiah owed the bank over three-hundred-thousand dollars. And when he couldn't borrow any more..."

Noem raised a hand, silencing her. "I can pretty much guess he took out loans from men like that fella that just paid us a little visit."

Lavinia shivered. *"Ja."*

"A lot of men came around after Josiah passed," Abram continued. "We thought we'd paid them all. But it looks like there are still a few crawling out of the woodwork."

"No man worth his salt would take advantage of a widow," Gabriel interjected. "Some men have no self-respect."

Face taking on a stern expression, Noem's lips momentarily flattened. "If one fella found

Lavinia, others might come looking. But next time we won't be caught unawares."

Shuddering, Lavinia buried her face in her hands. She'd only made matters worse by trying to conceal her shame. Josiah still rested in an uneasy grave. Worse, by not telling the truth, she'd put her new *familie* in danger.

"I made a terrible mistake." From deep inside, a sob broke through her lips. "I shouldn't have married you, Noem."

So there it was. The truth was out.

Noem sat in silence. Having heard the details Lavinia had finally found the courage to share, he wasn't sure how to react. He didn't know Josiah had a gambling problem or that the man's addiction had left his wife and child teetering on the edge of bankruptcy. True, whispers had gone around that Josiah had some association with dishonest men. But no one had specifically come out and pointed a definitive finger.

Now that he had the facts, he understood his new bride's reluctance to put her heart on the line a second time. Josiah had lied to her, destroying everything she'd believed in. Instead of protecting her, he'd recklessly gambled away their security and the very roof that sheltered them. The Bible cautioned against luck and chance in the pursuit of profit. The craving for wealth gained hastily had dropped many a man to his knees.

Lavinia continued, breaking the silence that had fallen between them. "I should have told you before we wed."

A dull throb kicked behind Noem's eyes, but he ignored the discomfort. All he needed was a little rest and he'd be fine. "I don't blame you for not wanting to talk about it. No one likes to speak ill of loved ones who have passed." Rising from his seat, he closed the distance between them, and then reached for her hands.

Lavinia flinched, backing away. She looked close to sobbing, her expression crumbling into misery. "I don't deserve any forgiveness for deceiving you." Tears rimmed her eyes and trekked down her cheeks. "That man could have killed you, and it would have been my fault."

Barely able to bear her anguish, Noem tried again. Catching her hands, he cradled them between his. Her skin was cold to the touch. Looking into her beautiful face, so pale and drawn, he saw only conflict. Misery and regret simmered in the depths of her eyes.

"That didn't happen. I got roughed up a little, but I'd gladly do it again to keep you safe."

Pale but controlled, she tipped back her head. "You're not angry?"

He offered a smile. "*Nein*. And I'm still pleased you married me. I wouldn't have it any other way."

A shudder went through her. "You are too *gut* for me."

"Oh, I have my moments. Trust me when I say I was ready to swing that hoe. But I knew I'd hurt that man." He shook his head. "I didn't want you or the *youngies* to see anything like that coming from me, so I held my temper."

"He might have had it from me if he'd have kept comin'," Gabriel muttered under his breath.

"I feel part of this is my fault," Abram said, stepping into the conversation. "I should have said something. But I didn't feel it was my place to share Lavinia's business."

"I appreciate you didn't talk out of place, Minister," Gabriel said. "You were only doin' what you thought was right."

"As a man of the church, maybe that's so. As your *schwager*, I should have told you."

Lavinia's pale cheeks reddened. "I thought I'd paid everyone who'd come around saying Josiah owed them money. I was willing to give every penny I had to make those horrible men go away."

"You paid the men what they said they

were owed," Abram countered. "That was fair enough."

Replaying the confrontation in his mind, Noem recalled a snippet the *Englischer* had tossed out. "That fellow said he'd been in jail when Josiah passed. Having that information can help the police identify him."

Abram nodded. "We should get into town. Each minute we wait means he gets farther away."

"I agree," Gabriel added. "I'll be here to keep an eye while you're gone." As he pulled back his shoulders, a glint came into his eyes. "I might be old, but I can handle a scuffle. That scallywag better watch himself."

"I think I've had enough scuffling for one day," Noem said.

Lavinia reached for Jesse. "*Danke*, Abram, for coming to give us a warning. I can't imagine what the people who bought the house must think. I imagine they were just trying to be helpful when they told him where I'd gone."

Abram pursed his lips. "I'm glad they let us know. I'm just sorry I didn't get here before he got away. I left as soon as I found out."

Seeing the conflict in his face set Noem to thinking. "If we had a phone here, you could have called."

"*Ja*, true," Abram allowed.

"I'm considering investing in a cell phone."

"The *Ordnung* does allow them," Abram confirmed. "Bishop Graber carries one himself, for business purposes."

Conflict darkened the old man's brow. "Not sure I'd agree with havin' them in the house."

Noem held up his hands. "I'm not suggesting anything fancy. Just a couple of flip phones. We're allowed radios for news and weather reports, so I don't see the difference."

Chin jutting, Gabriel doubled down. "Once you start allowin' one thing, others start creepin' in."

Sensing the stubborn streak coming out in his parent, Noem dug in his heels. He'd do whatever it took to keep his *familie* safe. He didn't feel he was caving to *Englisch* ways, but rather being sensible.

"It'd be different if we lived in town where we had some neighbors to help," he pointed out. "But when you and I go to work, Lavinia's here all by herself with three *youngies*. What if one of them got hurt? By the time she got to the phone box down the road…" He shook his head. "Well, I don't even want to think about that."

"We're not *Englisch*. We don't need to be takin' on their ways," Gabriel insisted.

Assuming the mantle of a peacemaker, Abram stepped up. "Now hold on. You both have valid points. But in this case, I'm going to say you need to err on the side of caution. The world's not safe. And *Gott* warns us not to be foolish and have care where we walk. I've gotten a couple of phones for my *familie*. Maddie's close to delivering. If she goes into labor, she'll be able to call for help."

"If the bishop allows it, I'd say it's fine to have one as long as we don't abuse the privilege." Noem turned to his *ehefrau*. "What do you think?"

Surprised to be invited into the conversation, Lavinia demurred. "Josiah would never allow me to have one."

Her reply brought Noem up short. "Josiah isn't making the decision," he countered in a gentle tone. "You are. How do you feel about the need?" Amish men didn't hesitate to consult their wives about matters that would affect the home and *youngies*. True, a man made the final call, but not before listening to what the womenfolk had to say.

Tightening her hold on the *boppli*, Lavinia glanced toward Penelope and Sophie. As they were distracted in play, their fright had passed. Conflict and concern warred in her expression. "I would feel safer having one."

"Then that's what we're going to do," he decided. "After I report the incident, Abram and I will pick up a couple of phones."

"I guess my opinions don't mean nothin'," Gabriel grumbled.

Noem put his foot down. "This is something I'm not going to argue about. It's a matter of safety. It probably wouldn't hurt for you to carry one, too."

Bushy brows knitted fiercely. "Why, I'd never—"

Abram tipped his head. "The Lord counsels us that the prudent sees danger and does his best to avoid it. If a phone allows you to avoid trouble, then I would say it's well worth having."

Gabriel rubbed a hand across his bearded face. "*Ach*, using *Gott*'s word to change my mind."

Abram chuckled. "That is the advantage of being a minister. The Bible does say we are to prepare our minds for action."

"I suppose puttin' one in my pocket wouldn't hurt matters."

"If I needed to reach you, I could," Noem added. "You don't even have to answer it. Just check your texts."

Lavinia gave an anxious look. "I don't care for devices myself. I'd only use it when necessary."

"I suppose that'd be acceptable," the old man allowed.

Relieved he'd gotten an agreement from all sides, Noem felt his tension thaw. The resolution was an acceptable one. Knowing he'd be in reach eased his mind.

"If we're going to get this done, we should get going," Abram prodded. "You up for the ride, Noem? You still look a little pale."

Noem gently probed his aching temple. His scraped skin burned. An odd pressure pulsed behind his eyes, but the discomfort was tolerable. He would have liked a chance to lie down and rest, but that wasn't possible.

"Let me change my shirt and we'll go. No reason to show up looking like I got kicked into the dirt."

Returning his hat to his head, Abram nodded. "I'll wait in my buggy."

"I washed your shirts this morning," Lavinia said, hurrying to fetch a fresh garment from her laundry basket. "They're dry now, but I haven't had time to iron them."

"*Danke.* Don't suppose a few wrinkles matter."

Shirt in hand, he headed to the spare washroom. After closing the door and changing his shirt, he filled the basin with water and pressed a washcloth to his skin. The warmth helped soothe the ache. Glancing into the mirror, he angled his head to look at the large bruise that had formed.

"He got the best of me," he murmured. Nevertheless, he was satisfied with how he'd handled the matter. The other man had thrown the first punch, giving him leave to defend himself. In that regard, his conscience was clear, and he didn't believe the Lord would judge him harshly. Once he'd reported the assault, the police would be tasked with taking over.

Finished cleaning up, Noem brushed a few strands of hair over the wound. Tucking his shirt in, he rejoined the others. His *daed* and Lavinia were in the kitchen.

Coffee in hand, Gabriel sat at the kitchen table. Lavinia fussed with Jesse, coaxing the *boppli* to take his meal. The *boi* wasn't happy, batting her hand away.

"*Ach*, he just isn't hungry," she exclaimed, setting aside his bottle.

Noem didn't have a chance to comment. Sophie and Penelope gave him a nervous look. Their half fearful, half curious expressions drew his attention.

"It's all right. The bad man has gone."

"I was scared," Penelope whispered, as if afraid to speak louder.

Noem bent to her level. "I know. But he won't be coming back."

"Promise?"

"*Ja.* You have my word."

Sophie curiously touched his temple. "That bad boo-boo." Leaning forward, she pressed a sloppy kiss to his bruised skin. "Make it all better."

Noem touched his cheek. An intense rush of emotion surged through him. "It does. *Danke.*" He opened his arms and pulled them close. Knowing these precious little souls viewed him as a parental figure filled him with pride.

He'd give everything to protect them.

Even his own life.

Chapter Twelve

Close to pulling her hair out, Lavinia dashed around the kitchen. Most every morning in the household was filled with activity, but Sundays were especially busy when there was a church service to attend. Getting five people up, fed and dressed in time to leave entailed a lot of coordination. Despite her intention to have each minute timed, some mishap or another threw her off schedule. Not ten minutes after she'd gotten breakfast on the table, Jesse needed his diaper changed. A minute later, Penelope dumped her cereal on her lap. Sophie trailed in her wake, whimpering to be held.

Shoving the last bite of toast in his mouth, Noem pushed away from the table. "Hand Jesse here and I'll get him taken care of." Dressed in trousers and a white shirt, his suspenders dangled around his waist. His stubble had thickened, mossing the lower part of his face with the beginnings of a beard. The addition of facial hair had entirely changed his look, maturing his boyish features. Concealed beneath the locks of his long hair, the bruise marring his temple was barely noticeable.

Offering a smile, she handed the *boppli* over. *"Danke."* Cutting a glance at the clock, she winced. Time was ticking away, and she'd not had a second to see after her own needs.

Nephew in hand, Noem cocked his hand toward the messy little girls. "I'll help Penelope change, too."

Bending, Lavinia scooped up Sophie. "You don't mind?" she asked, pressing a hand against her toddler's forehead to check for fever. A virus had been going around and it was better to be safe than sorry.

He chuckled. "I think I've gotten the hang of things. I'm sure I can get her into something clean."

"Her blue dress is in the second drawer."

"Got it," Noem said, heading toward the nursery so he could use the changing table. *"Daed* should have the buggy ready. We'll need to leave soon if we're going to be on time."

"I'll get changed, too." Lavinia carried Sophie into her bedroom and lay the toddler on her bed. She closed the door for a bit of privacy.

"Now sit quietly while *Mamm* changes."

Sophie flopped down on the quilt. "Mmm, 'kay." Humming, she clapped in time to her tune.

Lavinia smiled at her little one. Like most *kinder*, Sophie was flexible to life's changes. She'd taken to Penelope and Jesse, accepting both as her siblings. True, Sophie had her moments of fussiness, clinging closer than usual. But that was normal, especially for the child in the middle. Lavinia had done her best to divide her attention equally but wasn't always successful. It helped that Noem was taking on more responsibilities. He often took care of the *youngies* without being asked, lending a hand to change a diaper or give Jesse his evening bath.

Noem's so different from Josiah. The two men were like night and day.

Outgoing, brash and a bit of a braggart, Josiah was all about appearances. He liked having nice things and showing them off. Didn't matter that he couldn't afford them; he'd worry about the debt another day.

Noem was the complete opposite. Quiet and thoughtful, he plodded like a trusty old mule. If she mentioned something needed to be done around the house, he simply went and did it. There was no argument, no putting it off for another day.

Eyes brimming, she blinked hard. When she'd married Noem out of desperation, she'd been terrified to tell him the truth about Josiah's gambling. Thankfully, he hadn't blamed her when the ugly narrative had revealed itself. He'd simply gone to the police station and reported the incident. He managed the matter quietly and with little fanfare. When others inquired about his injury, he'd shrugged it off, saying he'd been careless at work.

Realizing she'd fallen into the past again, she gave her head a little shake. "You're dallying, Lavinia."

Stepping to her armoire, she selected her best dress. Like most Amish women, she didn't have a large wardrobe. A few dresses for daily wear and housework, a nicer frock for Sunday services and special events, and her widow's weeds turned wedding dress was all she owned. She'd discarded the dress she'd worn when she'd wed Josiah. It was cut from a lovely piece of rose-shaded fabric, and she had donated it to a thrift shop. There was no reason for it to take up space. Josiah was gone. The life they'd shared was in ashes.

She twirled her unruly curls into a bun and pinned on her *kapp*. A glance in the mirror revealed that her face was a bit pale. She gave her cheeks a pinch to bring some color to her face.

"Lavinia? We need to get going."

"Coming, Noem!" she called back. Giving herself a last nervous check, she scooped Sophie off the bed. "Time to go."

Sophie grinned from ear to ear. "Pretty Mommy."

"Pretty girl," she cooed back.

Noem waited in the living room. Having changed Jesse, he'd gotten Penelope into fresh clothes. Nearing five, she was old enough to wear an apron and *kapp*. She looked adorable and had taken to Amish life the way a duck took to water. Developing well for her age, she had a curious mind. Eager to learn, she willingly did her chores, relishing the praise her efforts earned.

A smile widened his mouth. "I don't think I've seen you in that dress before."

"I only wear it for church."

"You look lovely."

A blush warmed her cheeks. "You owe me no compliment. I look the same way I always do."

"A man has a right to be proud of his *ehefrau*."

Embarrassed, Lavinia looked down at the tips of her plain boots. "You got no bargain in me," she countered to deflect the compliment.

"You're wrong. You are more precious to me than any jewel."

"You'd better have a care with such flattery."

His expression didn't dim. "I'm only speaking the truth."

She eyed him back. "And if I were to speak the truth, I'd have to say it looks like you've forgotten to finish yourself." She cocked a brow toward his dangling suspenders.

"Sorry." Noem placed Jesse in his travel seat, then pulled the straps around his shoulders. The material of his shirt stretched across his chest, emphasizing the tautness of his muscular frame. Suspenders in place, he slipped into a simple black coat. A black stovepipe hat finished his outfit. All in all, his finery was smartly worn. "Better?"

Taking in the length of him, Lavinia nodded. The subtle changes he'd recently undergone suddenly came together. A bit on the thin side when they'd wed, he'd filled out, putting on weight and muscle. His voice, too, had taken on a pleasing timbre. He no longer resembled the pale, uncertain fellow who'd shown up on her doorstep. A strong, confident man stood in his place.

"*Ja*. Can't show up to church half-dressed," she laughed. "That would surely set tongues to wagging."

"I suppose it would." Shouldering Jesse's travel bag, Noem picked up the *boppli* before ushering everyone toward the door. "We'll just about make it on time if we leave now."

"*Ach*, I almost forgot the food." She dashed to the counter and claimed her offering for the luncheon that would take place once services had ended. A bit rushed, she'd baked up a basketful of pigs in a blanket: thin slices of ham and cheese rolled into sourdough and baked golden brown. Basket on her arm, she ushered Penelope and Sophie in front of her.

Gabriel waited in the driveway. He usually preferred an open-style buggy with a back-end bed for hauling cargo. But this morning he'd chosen a sleek black model, complete with a roof, sliding side door and a front windshield. Designed to carry at least half a dozen people, it provided a comfortable ride.

"Been years since we've used this one," Noem commented, lifting Penelope and Sophie into the back seat.

"Not since Amelia passed," the old man confirmed. "I was thinkin' I might sell it, but it looks like it'll be worth holdin' on to."

"Glad you changed your mind."

The old man's craggy face softened. "Didn't think we'd ever have a real *familie* again."

"*Gott* had other plans." Noem chuckled, buckling the girls in before setting Jesse's safety seat on the floor, facing it to the rear as he would if they were riding in a car. He took great care to make sure the *youngies* were settled in. Though the Amish were not required to use seat belts, many newer models included them as an added feature. After stowing Jesse's bag, he held out a hand. "Up you go, my lady."

Accepting his help, Lavinia climbed inside. She sat her basket on her lap, careful to keep the food covered with a cloth. *"Danke."*

Noem took a seat beside his *daed*. "Looks like we're ready."

"Giddyap!" Gabriel gave the horse a tap with the reins, setting the buggy into motion. Making a quick turn, the horse trotted down the gravel drive. Minutes later, they were rolling over the asphalt highway at a steady clip.

More than a little nervous, Lavinia glanced out the passenger-side window. Today was the first time they would attend church since they'd wed. Rather than traveling to a dedicated building, individual families hosted services at their homes. Divided into districts based on location, a typical gathering had about thirty families, each with two or three ministers and several deacons. Larger communities often had more than one bishop. Folks living outside the city limits usually joined the closest neighbor who'd volunteered to host. As she'd wed Noem, she'd also joined his congregation. Some folks she would know from school and social events in town. Others, not so much. She looked forward to making new friends.

Geoff and Ruth Stutz stood ready to greet their guests. Their property was wide and sprawling and included a voluminous barn. Earlier in the morning, the deacons had arrived to set up benches and put out the hymnals. These moved from one home to another via a large wagon to accommodate worshippers. Services were followed by a potluck meal and games.

Rolling up, Gabriel found a place to park. "Looks like the pews will be full today." Catching sight of Wanetta Graff standing amid the group, he grinned. "I sure hope she brought her cinnamon rolls. Those are my favorites."

Noem nudged his *daed*. "Seems to me you and Wanetta are building a nice friendship. Maybe you ought to ask her on a walkabout."

The rough old man guffawed with embarrassment. "Why, I'd never— She was Amelia's best friend."

"I don't think *Mamm* would mind. You and Wanetta finding a little happiness would make her smile."

"Don't go puttin' the cart before the horse."

"I'm just giving you something to think about."

Gabriel scrubbed at his mouth. "I like Wanetta's cookin', is all. And she knows a lot about gardenin'. Doesn't hurt to listen to what she's got to say."

Noem chuckled. "I suppose not." After sliding open the door, he jumped down from his seat. "Guess we'd better not keep *Gott* waiting."

Forcing herself to relax, Lavinia stepped onto the ground. A few heads swiveled their way.

Lord, give me strength.

Smiling, she offered a nod to the people she knew. Most waved back in a friendly way.

Wanetta flagged her hand, a signal for her to join the group. "Lavinia," she called. "Come talk with us."

Seeing so many smiling faces made Lavinia's stress drain away. Pulling back her shoulders, she prepared to greet the group. She had an *ehmann* and two new little ones to call her own. She was no longer the Widow Simmons, but Mrs. Noem Witzel. She refused to allow herself to be shamed by Josiah's secrets any longer. His sin was his own to bear, and he would be the one to answer to his Maker.

Feeling blessed, she sent up a quick prayer. You've given me so much, Lord. I dare not ask for more.

* * *

Born and raised in the Plain community, Noem had spent a lot of time sitting in the pews. Gatherings were only held every other Sunday, and the Amish took their time to worship seriously. Services were three hours, sometimes longer, depending on the enthusiasm of the ministers preaching.

In past times, he'd usually give the speakers half an ear, listening without much interest. As he saw it, he didn't have anything to repent for. He went about his business without causing anyone any trouble. He thought he was a *gut* person.

He was wrong.

The Lord had recently opened his eyes, showing him the reflection of a man who was selfish and self-centered.

But that man was no more.

The realization that he could do better—that he must do better—had shaken him to his core. He called himself a Christian, but he hadn't acted like one for a long time. There were other people in this world. People with wounded hearts and fragile spirits. People who needed shelter from the storms of life.

Taking an *ehefrau* devoted to the Lord made it impossible to turn a blind eye. Without fail, Lavinia studied her daily devotional, giving her time and attention to the Lord. Her weekly sewing group also engaged in a Bible study. His *daed*, too, was a faithful reader.

When she'd invited him to join the evening sit-down, Noem had reluctantly agreed. He'd always found the Bible to be a dry bit of reading. But his thoughts changed once he'd recognized the true nature of the book. It wasn't just history; it was *His story.* Not only was it the narrative of the Creator, but it was also a record of events—a written testament of civilization. That alone made it fascinating. Religion was not just an abstract idea, but a way to grow closer to *Gott*, to truly know Him in all His glory.

A sharp elbow jabbed him in the side.

"Your mind's wanderin'," Gabriel whispered under his breath. "You're supposed to be singin'."

Startled, Noem bowed his head. "Sorry."

He glanced at the hymnal in his hands. The *Ausbund* was a collection of songs going back to the beginning of the Anabaptist movement. Written in German, the tunes had been handed down through many generations. Normally, he didn't have any problem reading the small print. Now he could barely see it. His vision was a little blurry.

He rubbed his eyes with his thumb and forefinger. Feeling a bit disoriented, he gave himself a shake. Following his run-in with the trespasser, he'd been having trouble seeing clearly. A haze hovered around the edges of objects, making it hard to focus. Headaches had also begun to plague him, leaving him shaky and out of sorts. Some days they weren't so bad. Other times, they were painful and unrelenting, shredding his ability to function. Aspirin helped dull the ache, but the thud behind his temples never entirely went away.

Suspecting he'd suffered a mild concussion during the fight, he'd kept his complaints to himself. No reason to upset Lavinia. She already blamed herself enough for the stranger's intrusion into their lives. As a safety precaution, he'd also purchased the cell phones. And once he'd learned the bishop carried one, too, Gabriel had decided owning such a device was acceptable.

Unable to focus on the small print, Noem pretended to sing. Usually, he found the sound of voices joined in praise quite lovely. Today the harmonies set his nerves on edge, like fingernails dragging across a chalkboard.

I'm just stressed. Too much to think about. Everything's going to be fine.

Hymn ending, one of the ministers stepped forward to preach. An older man in his fifties,

Daniel Zerbe spoke with a folksy, meandering style. His sermons often stretched on for an hour, sometimes longer.

Content to listen, Noem sat in rapt attention. The homily touched on many things he'd once questioned, leading him to believe the Lord did indeed reach out through those men he'd called to speak on His behalf. Caught in the grip of the Lord's word, Noem found that the hours passed in the blink of an eye. After the preaching ended, Bishop Graber arrived to speak and share news from other church districts. The Amish population was growing, and the bishop had four congregations to visit throughout the morning.

By the time the last notes of the closing hymn faded, everyone was ready for a break. Deacons gathered the hymn books and benches and tucked them back into a specially built wagon.

Glad for a chance to stretch his legs, Noem stood. "*Gut* service."

"Been a long time since I appreciated *Gott*'s wisdom," Gabriel commented. Smiling, he cocked his head toward the bright sky. "I feel like the Lord's showin' me your *mamm* and Callie are at peace. They'll be fine until I join them."

"*Ja.* But don't count on passing too soon.

You've got *enkelkinder.* They expect their *grobvater* to be there and see them grow."

"I intend to." Gabriel's expression changed to one of shame. "I know I've said it before, but I'll say it again. I'm sorry I acted like a grumpy mule when you told me you'd be takin' Callie's *youngies.*"

"You weren't exactly the most pleasant fellow about it."

"Didn't seem like anything about it would work. Truth be told, I'd gotten used to stewin' in my misery and didn't want to change it."

"I'd say *Gott* sent us a blessing we both needed."

"Amen." Catching sight of Wanetta, Gabriel slicked back his hair before setting his hat on his head. "Think I'll ask Wanetta if she'll sit with me for lunch. I heard Ruth's servin' meatloaf and mashed potatoes, so it'll be worth stayin' for."

"I think that's a fine idea."

Usually, Gabriel skipped the meal and the socializing. Today he was talkative, greeting people with a handshake. The chill of grief had finally loosened its hold. The older man had realized there was life after death. It was all right to go on and seek a fresh start.

Glancing across the aisle, Noem caught sight of Lavinia standing among a group of her friends. As she cradled Jesse in her arms, her eyes were bright and a smile lit her expression. The women fussed over the *boppli*. Penelope and Sophie, too, got their share of attention. Clad in matching dresses, the little girls looked adorable. A few of the older widows could be overheard telling Lavinia it was *gut* sense for her to remarry while she still had her looks.

Ears burning, Noem stepped away so he wouldn't be caught eavesdropping. He couldn't have asked for a finer woman to be his help-mate. When the entire situation had seemed doomed from the beginning, she'd held firm, binding the household together with her unwavering faith.

Unsure whether it would be appropriate to bother Lavinia while she was visiting, he hung back.

Find something to do. Be helpful.

Noem grabbed a bench and carried it toward the waiting wagon. "Here you go."

David Lochman relieved him of its weight. *"Danke."* Beefy, broad and strong as an ox, David worked at the local feed mill.

Noem handed over his prayer book. "Is there anything else I can do?"

David tucked the slender volume among others stacked in a small chest. *"Nein.* We're done."

Leaving the wagon behind, the two walked

to join the others. The Stutz property buzzed with activity. Overseeing lunch, Ruth directed the other women with an experienced hand. Once they set up the tables, they carried out plate after plate loaded with food. The older folks had sought the shade from the overhanging limbs of tall trees to swap a little gossip. Eager for some good old-fashioned fun, other people were organizing games. Hankering to burn off some energy, a group of younger men tossed a football back and forth.

One called out, tossing the ball. "David— catch!"

Laughing, David caught the ball. "Getting up a game?"

"*Ja*. We could use a few more."

David cocked his head toward Noem. "You up for a skirmish?"

Surprised to be invited, Noem hesitated. Several of the fellas playing ball had teased him unmercifully about his stutter when they were back in school. However, quite a few years had passed. The boys had grown into men. Maybe it was time to give them the benefit of doubt and let go of old grievances. Committing to living by *Gott*'s word meant he had to continue making changes in himself.

If I don't forgive them, how can I expect the Lord to forgive me?

"I'll play." A headache still banged behind his eyes, but a little exercise and fresh air might help clear his head. He blinked again, trying to evade the black spots floating in front of his eyes. If the problem persisted, he'd visit an ophthalmologist. Perhaps he'd reached an age when he needed glasses.

David clapped him on the shoulder. "*Gut* man. Let's show them how it's done."

Breaking into teams, the players assumed their positions. The Amish played a tamer version of football, more akin to rugby, with each side trying to advance the ball toward designated goalposts. The team with the ball made the initial rush, attempting to dodge members of the opposing side. If the player carrying the ball was tagged out, he had a few seconds to pass it to his closest teammate. If all players were tagged out before reaching the end zone, the ball changed sides.

Someone whistled, signaling the start of the game. The players rushed forward.

Noem ran with the rest of his team, doing his best to block the advancing players from tackling their man carrying the ball. The game was spirited and moved fast. Several players were quickly tagged out.

The game continued, growing more competitive.

Heart beating double time, Noem was vaguely aware of a sudden change in his body. Limbs going numb, dizziness washed through his senses.

Something's wrong.

Gripped by panic, he struggled to halt his forward momentum. Seconds ticked by, but his body did nothing he commanded it to. He turned desperately, struggling, falling to his knees. He tried to rise, but his arms and legs were useless, sending him into a full-length sprawl. A burst of lightning exploded inside his skull, sending a jolt through his entire system. His vision abruptly dimmed, flickering alarmingly before completely blanking out.

Blinded, he was vaguely aware of voices calling his name. Someone gave him a shake. Unable to respond, he lay helpless. His inability to move bewildered him, sending a rush of adrenaline jetting through his veins. But he couldn't respond. Not even to cry out for help. As if he were hanging on a crumbling ledge, his tenuous hold on reality began to give way.

Losing his grip, he plunged into an abyss of unconsciousness.

Chapter Thirteen

Fighting his way out of the darkness, Noem struggled back toward consciousness. Opening his eyes, he was aware he was awake. But he couldn't see. As if staring into a thickly clouded sky, a gray-white haze blanketed his vision.

Alarmed, he struggled to sit up. By the feel of the mattress beneath him, he knew he was lying on a bed. Cocking his head, he heard strange noises all around, unfamiliar sounds and faraway voices. An odor that smelled clean, cold and sterile scented the air.

Gentle hands caught his shoulders, pressing him back. "Don't try to get up," a familiar voice said.

Noem resisted. Anxiety rising, his heart thudded double time in his chest. "Wh-what's going on?" Half frightened and confused, he pushed out the words in a rush. "I can't see." His hand flailed, reaching for comfort.

Small warm hands wrapped around his. "I'm here."

Shaking his head, Noem tried to orient himself. It was strange looking out of eyes that wouldn't focus. "I can't see," he repeated. "My eyes aren't working."

Lavinia's grip tightened. "I can't imagine how frightening that must be."

Mind fuzzed, Noem turned his head every which way. "Where are we?"

"We're in Sparta, at the medical center. They let me ride in the ambulance with you."

"Ambulance?"

"Ja." A pause. "Don't you remember?"

Noem searched his memory. A series of far-away images tumbled through his mind. After crashing to the ground, he was vaguely aware of people gathering around him. Past that, his senses had blanked out.

A rural community, Humble offered little in the way of medical services. The small clinic staffed by a general practitioner only provided rudimentary care. Accidents such as broken limbs or other devastating injuries had to be sent on to the next town, which was over thirty miles away.

"Nein. A little here and there, but not much."

"You passed out. The doctors in the emergency room were concerned when they couldn't get you to wake up. They ran a lot of tests. We're waiting to see what they have to say."

Concerned he'd caused so much trouble, Noem cocked his head. "Where are the *youngies*? And *Daed*? Are they here?"

"Gabriel took the *kinder* home. My *familie* has gone to help him." She hurried to explain. "And Bishop Graber is waiting in the lobby. He had his driver follow the ambulance so we would have a ride home."

Sorting through the information, Noem squinted hard. If only his eyes would focus. But the blur lingered, blanking out most everything. "How long have we been here?"

"Hours."

He licked papery lips. Not exactly the way to enjoy a warm spring day. After church, he'd wanted to spend the afternoon putting together a playhouse set he'd purchased, a surprise for the *youngies*. He'd looked forward to seeing Penelope and Sophie enjoying the swings and slide. He'd also gotten up the nerve to approach his *daed* about adding extra rooms to the existing house. If Gabriel agreed to the additions, Noem wanted to sketch out a few ideas. One way or another, they would have a bigger house, with room for their *familie* to grow.

He blinked again, inwardly cursing the haze obstructing his vision. "I don't understand what happened. Why can't I see?"

"The doctor hasn't let us know anything yet."

"Surely they've learned something by now."

"I told them about the fight." Lavinia's voice trembled as she spoke. "They said you could have an injury that's just now showing up."

That made sense. During the fight, he'd taken a nasty blow. It probably hadn't been a wise idea not to seek medical attention. Now he'd have to suffer the consequences of his foolish decision. He should have known something was wrong when the headaches persisted.

Forcing himself to relax, Noem lay back. His head connected with a soft pillow. Shifting in place, he felt a blanket rub against his legs. He realized they had replaced his regular clothes with a thin short gown.

Oh, my...

"I guess the phones we got came in handy."

"Most all the younger folks had one. I'm thankful now the *Ordnung* allows us to use them for emergencies."

"I didn't mean to cause anyone any worry."

"Everyone's praying for a complete healing."

Noem turned his head, staring into blank

nothingness. Emotion squeezed his throat. Though he wanted to believe faith would be enough to carry them through the challenging times, he was also realistic enough to know that what a person prayed for and what *Gott* delivered were two different things.

The sound of a door opening interrupted their conversation.

"Good to see you're awake, Mr. Witzel," a male voice greeted. "I'm Doctor Gundersen."

Noem offered a nod. "*Gut* to meet you, Doctor."

"You gave everyone a pretty bad scare," Gundersen continued briskly. "How are you feeling?"

Noem placed his palm against his forehead. "I've got a headache. And my eyes aren't working right."

"Oh? Can you explain?"

"My sight's gone dim," Noem replied, struggling to find the words.

"Mmm. Are you able to see light or make out any shapes?"

"*Ja.* I see light. It's like I'm looking through gauze or something like that." Rubbing his eyes, he concentrated. "Nothing else is coming through. It's just one big white blur."

"I'd like to say that surprises me, but it doesn't." Gundersen shuffled some papers. "I have the results of your CT scan from Radiology. I don't want you to be alarmed, but the initial results show that you have a brain tumor. Speech issues, loss of balance and blindness are just a few of the symptoms that can occur."

Heart skipping a beat, Noem felt his blood pressure drop. The single word was a painful shattering shock, like a stone flung through a pane of glass. Veins filling with ice, he could only focus on that one dreadful word: *tumor.*

Lavinia tightened her grip on his hand. "Is it cancer?"

"It's too early to give a definitive diagnosis. Additional tests are going to be needed." Gundersen shuffled more papers. "I know it's frightening for you and your loved ones, but once we know what we're looking at, there are options for treatment."

Floundering, Noem struggled to keep his composure. Falling into despair wouldn't help anything. As the head of his household, it was up to him to be strong, to make the decisions that would benefit his *ehefrau* and *youngies*. When he'd wed Lavinia, he'd believed they would have a long future together. Given his diagnosis and the potential outcome, the promise of tomorrow had vanished.

"Can it be removed?"

"As this is not my area of expertise, I'm not

going to give you an answer," Gundersen countered. "I'm going to refer you to a specialist who is better equipped to handle this sort of medical issue."

"Does this have anything to do with the injury I got last week?"

Lavinia tightened her clasp on him. "I told you about the man who attacked Noem," she added, filling in the details a second time.

"I'm afraid I got the worst of it." Noem pressed his hand against his left temple. "I got a pretty hard kick."

"Did you see anyone about it?" Gundersen asked.

"*Nein.* It didn't seem that bad. I've had some headaches—"

"I'm afraid your decision to tough it out might not have been the best course of action," Gundersen said, interrupting. "But it's doubtful the injury aggravated the tumor."

"Then there's a chance I've had this thing in my head a long t-time?"

"Possibly. Brain tumor diagnosis is often incidental. Most are usually found while examining the individual for another reason, such as a head injury or other neurologic problem." Pausing, he added. "I've also noticed that you stutter now and again."

"*Ja.* I have m-most of my life."

"That's often a giveaway there might be an issue inside the brain. I am going to assume it was never checked when you were a child."

"*Nein.* It was just something I lived with. But the more you talk, the worse it s-sounds."

"Before you panic, you need to know not all tumors are malignant," Gundersen said. "Some people go through a lifetime never knowing they had one. It might have gone undiscovered for years if you hadn't gotten in a fight that day. As for the concussion part, it takes about two weeks to recover. You shouldn't have been engaging in any kind of sport or other physical activity sooner than one week from sustaining the injury."

"I was worried the injury was worse than we thought," Lavinia interjected. A faint shiver passed through her.

Sensing her rising emotion, Noem tugged her hand. "Look at it as a blessing in disguise," he said, doing his best to soothe her worry. "If nothing had happened now, it might have been worse later on down the road."

"The sooner a tumor is discovered, the easier it is to deal with," Gundersen added.

"Is there any chance that thing in my head will fix itself? You know, just go back to being the w-way it was?"

Gundersen cleared his throat. "You can certainly choose to take a wait-and-see approach. But the longer you wait, the worse it could get. Delaying treatment too long might mean you pass the point of viable options for any recovery."

The doctor's warning echoed in his mind.

Noem's blood ran cold. "Are you saying I could be blind for the rest of my life—or possibly d-die?"

"I'm not going to answer one way or another," Gundersen continued. "The truth is, with tumors we simply don't have all the data. And I know that as one of the Amish, you may be reluctant to seek treatment. I'm aware Plain folks believe that medicine helps, but God alone heals."

Noem struggled to keep his rising panic at bay. The idea that he might be blind forever frightened him. He was a man who made a living with his hands, working with components that required precise installation. Without his vision, he'd be worthless.

A multitude of ominous thoughts crowded into his brain, pecking away like a crow devouring carrion. What would happen if his sight wasn't restored? The question haunted him, a specter that refused to be banished. There was also the matter of the bills that would soon be coming in. Medical treatment was expensive. Like most Amish, he didn't have health insurance. And not a week before, he'd sunk every dime he'd saved into buying Zeb Yoder's shop. Though he owned a business, he no longer had a regular paycheck because he'd opted to take a draw—adjusting his compensation based on the performance and profits.

Overtaken by weariness, Noem closed his eyes. He felt hopeless, cast adrift in a sea of adversity. The future he'd envisioned with Lavinia drizzled away, slipping through his fingers like fine grains of sand.

The ride home was mostly silent. Devastated by the diagnosis Noem had received, Lavinia found herself unable to think about anything else. The day, so filled with fellowship and hope, had closed on a somber note.

After Doctor Gundersen had delivered the devastating news, there was little more to be done. Saying he would be in touch about an appointment with a specialist, Gundersen had released Noem from the hospital.

Noem could go home, but he was to rest and stay off his feet. He also wasn't to engage in any intense physical activity for at least a week. The attending physician didn't know how long it would take to arrange an appointment for Noem with a neurologist, but he promised to try to hurry the process along. If the tumor was cancerous, it could cause more damage.

Fighting to keep her composure, Lavinia glanced at her *ehmann*. Sitting beside her, Noem looked pale and drawn. Lines of worry etched his features and turned down his mouth. It was apparent that the diagnosis had deeply disturbed him.

Helpless, she forced herself to remain calm. Since their marriage, he had become her rock, her strength. The idea of losing him was unbearable. Fear lingered in the back of her mind. Stalking. Taunting. A malevolent presence that existed even in shadows, darker than the darkest night. Though the doctor hadn't said as much, a nagging fear warned her the tumor had the potential to be fatal.

Gott, *give me peace.* She recalled the soothing words of Peter, who advised the faithful to cast all anxieties upon the Lord.

As if he sensed her thoughts, Noem's fingers closed around hers. His grip, so strong, was welcome.

"I'm not afraid," he murmured, staring through wide-open sightless eyes.

Swallowing back the lump in her throat, Lavinia nodded. "*Gott* is with us."

Silence descended, broken only by the hum of the engine. Headlights penetrating the dark, the church van rolled down the highway.

The driver's voice interrupted. "Y'all mind if I turn on some music?"

The bishop gave his assent. "Not at all."

The driver turned the radio to a gospel station. "Okay?"

"Ja," Bishop Graber said.

"We should arrive in another twenty minutes," the driver said.

"Can't wait," Noem said and offered a wry laugh. "Hospitals aren't my favorite place to be."

The bishop chuckled, too. "No one wants to be there, I'm sure."

"Danke for staying. Lavinia and I both appreciate the help."

"Always happy to be of service."

Grateful for the bishop's support, Lavinia closed her eyes and focused on the music. The gentle lyrics of praise sent out a soothing message, bolstering her spirits. The songs were enriching, not only to the soul but to the heart as well.

Rewinding the events in her mind, she recalled Doctor Gundersen's diagnosis. The news he'd delivered was frightening. But that didn't mean Noem's tumor was incurable. Where there was life, there was hope. The Bible taught that faith was the assurance of things hoped for. Fate had dealt their *familie* another devastating blow. However, sinking into despair would accomplish nothing. Like the mighty oak, survival meant being strong enough to bend when the storms of adversity howled.

Opening her eyes, she looked at Noem. He was a well-built, solid man, and no one would ever suspect his health was anything but robust. But now his life hung in the balance. The tumor threatened to steal away everything.

Emotion gripped her lungs, forcing her to swallow past the tightness to breathe. Tears misted her vision. Drawn together by tragedy, she and Noem had married in haste and desperation. Friends who'd become strangers, they'd slowly become friends again. Friends who were on their way to becoming so much more. After a rocky start, they'd reached a bridge of understanding, ready to take the next steps toward tomorrow hand in hand. Now the abyss below threatened to snatch away everything they held dear.

Knowing tears would solve nothing, Lavinia swiped at her eyes. Gott *never promised us an easy walk*. The Lord did promise He would be there to see the weary traveler through to their destination. When she got home, she intended to reach out to everyone. A praying community was the strongest weapon against adversity, and she intended to use it.

Arriving on the outskirts of Humble, the driver turned off the highway. The short, twisty gravel road soon bought the welcome sight of home. Several buggies were parked in the drive.

"Looks like you've got company," the driver commented, shutting off the engine and headlights. Belching a little, the van settled into silence.

Noem felt around for the door handle and then opened the passenger-side door. "Didn't mean to cause a panic."

Lavinia slid out of the back seat. The day had been a long one, and she was exhausted. "I know everyone's worried." Taking Noem's arm, she guided him toward the house. "Have a care with your steps."

Noem tightened his grip. "It's strange to know where I am but not have my eyes to see it."

Joining them, Bishop Graber held the door open to allow entry into the screened-in veranda. "I pray *Gott* will return your vision soon."

Lavinia took Noem through the front door. A group of anxious faces greeted them. Aside from Gabriel and Wanetta, Abram and Maddie had come to sit with them. Annalise, too, was present, as were Samuel and Frannie.

Having taken it on herself to get supper on the table, Annalise worked diligently at the stove, preparing a simple meal. Bottle in hand, Maddie sat in the living room. Nestled in her loving arms, Jesse was perfectly content. Other members sat in a group, reading from the Bible. As prayer warriors, they had not hesitated to act on Noem's behalf.

"We made it," Bishop Graber announced. "Everyone is home, safe and sound."

"Thank the Lord," Gabriel exclaimed.

"We've been worried sick," Wanetta added.

Seeing Noem, Penelope and Sophie immediately rushed to offer hugs.

"*Dat* fall down," Sophie exclaimed, throwing her little arms around his legs.

Penelope burst into tears. "I was so scared you would go away."

Moving with care, Noem hunkered down. "Why is that?"

Penelope burbled, trying to speak through her anxiety. "Mamma went in the am—ambu, um, big truck," she explained, struggling to find the words. "She didn't come home. I was scared the doctor-man wouldn't let you go."

"Nothing could keep me away." Untangling himself from their hugs, Noem rose and took off his hat. "Would have been home sooner, but it took hours to get discharged. I think we spent most of our time sitting around, waiting to leave."

Lavinia kept her silence. That wasn't quite true, but there was no reason to refute his words. Though his diagnosis was a devastating one, he'd wanted to wait until they were home to share the worst of the news.

"Everyone's here," she whispered. "Do you feel like visiting, or would you like to go lie down?"

"If you don't mind, I'd like to sit at the table."

"All right." Lavinia guided him through the living room. "The table is directly in front of you."

Hat in hand, Bishop Graber followed. Welcoming his presence, the group greeted him with quiet, respectful nods.

Abram stepped forward, offering his hand. "Thank you for getting them home, Bishop."

James Graber returned the handshake. "Glad to do anything I can. My driver is available any time you need him." He reached in his pocket and pulled out his cell. "I'll give you his number, so you'll have it."

"Danke."

Rising, Gabriel pulled a chair away from

the table for Noem. "There's a place for you here, *sohn*."

Reaching out to find the chair, Noem sat. "Glad to get off my feet." Tipping back his head, he sniffed the air. "Correct me if I'm wrong, but I think I smell fresh coffee b-brewing."

Annalise grabbed a pot holder. "Coming right up." After filling a cup, she delivered it to the table. "I hope you're hungry. I'll have some food on the table in a minute."

"I could eat," Noem said, thanking her. "My stomach's been gnawing my backbone for an hour." He reached toward the center of the table. "Can someone lend a hand with the cream and sugar?"

Lavinia picked up a spoon. "Let me." She stirred in the extras. "Just the way you like it."

A stricken look crossed Gabriel's face. "I see it's true you've lost your sight."

Noem sipped his coffee. "Not entirely," he said after he'd lowered his cup. "I can see, but everything's blurry and out of focus, like I've got something wr-wrapped around my face."

"Was it because of the fight?" Abram asked.

"No, it had nothing to do with what's going on inside my head," Noem explained.

Face going chalk white, Gabriel leaned forward. "What did they say? Will your eyes work again?"

"They're not sure," Noem answered and gave a grim shake of his head. "The news isn't *gut*. I hate to say it, but there's a tumor."

Nerves strung tight, Lavinia listened as Noem explained what Doctor Gundersen had told him. There was no fear in his tone. Only calm resignation.

"The doctor said even if the tumor can be removed, there's no guarantee my sight will be restored. It could be something I'll have to live with through the time I have left on this earth—however long or short that may be."

"How do they plan to treat it?" Abram asked.

Sipping his coffee, Noem momentarily went silent. "I don't know. I'll have to see a specialist," he replied after a short pause. "But I'm not sure if I'll be going to see him."

Shocked, Lavinia felt herself go numb. "Of course you'll go."

Noem shook his head. "No, I won't." His chin set into a stubborn line. "Treatment's going to be expensive. I can't pay for it."

Consternation mingling in her emotions, Lavinia stared at him in dismay. How had he come to such a decision without speaking to her? His wasn't the only life that would be affected. Yes, it was true the Amish didn't believe in having insurance. But that didn't mean they didn't have resources. Plain folks believed it was the duty of the community and the church to care for one another.

"We'll find the money. There's a lot we can do." Auctions and bake sales were popular options for raising funds. Though Humble was a small community, it attracted *Englisch* visitors who were more than happy to pay for authentic Amish goods.

"I'm not sure it's worth the effort. Gundersen said there's no promise I'd get my sight back. I'm no doctor, either, but I know surgery like that would be mighty risky. Maybe it's best to put things in *Gott*'s hands and let it be."

Sitting quietly, Gabriel placed both his hands on the table. "I've got the money."

Noem's expression twisted into obstinacy. "You've worked your whole life to save it."

"Aye. And it was your *mamm* who made me put every spare cent away." The old man's voice trembled. "When I wanted to spend the money on finer things, she always put her foot down and said no. She was content to live a simple life knowing we had security."

"I remember Amelia always said the Lord blessed a simple life," Wanetta said, chuckling at the memory of her dear friend. "And I never knew her to go without. She would grow it, make it or trade for what she needed."

A tormented look flitted across Noem's face. "But *Mamm* didn't go to the doctor for what ailed her," he countered in a soft voice.

Gabriel's gaze simmered with regret. "No doctor could fix a broken heart. All your *mamm* ever wanted was for Callie to come back to the church so she could know her *enkelkinder*." Covering his face with his hands, the old man gave way to his grief. "I've lost Amelia. I've lost Callie. I can't stand losin' my only *sohn*." Suddenly, he slammed down a hand. "I won't, I tell you! I won't. *Gott* isn't callin' you home if I have anything to say about it!"

Caught by the grief in Gabriel's voice, Lavinia felt time swim out of focus, back to the day when Josiah died. The tragedy had struck repeated blows. Her life had crumbled, and she'd lost everything.

She fought to stifle her distress. *I'm not ready to lose him.* The idea of becoming a widow so soon after her second marriage was more than she could bear to face.

But the choice was his to make. She would abide by his decision. Even if it meant she would soon have to say goodbye.

"I'm willing to put my life in the Lord's

hands," Noem said and turned to the bishop. "Wouldn't that be right?"

Adjusting his glasses, Bishop Graber didn't hesitate. "It's true the Bible says prayer will heal the sick. However, I hope you will consider the fact that perhaps *Gott* also does His work by giving physicians the knowledge to aid in healing. *Gott* says mankind is His workmanship, created in Christ to do *gut* works."

"I agree," Abram added. "It would be foolish not to use the resources the Lord has provided."

"You have so much to lose and everything to gain," Bishop Graber said. "And you are needed, Noem."

And then there was silence. Emotions throughout the entire group were stretched to the breaking point.

"It's time to put that Witzel pride aside, *sohn*," Gabriel said. "Your *mamm* and Callie couldn't, and it put them in their graves." As he glanced toward Wanetta, his tense expression softened. "I let stubbornness keep me from livin'. I'm not doin' that anymore. I'm goin' to get out, and I'm goin' to live the life the Lord meant for me to have. You have a life, too, *sohn*. Live it. Even if you don't have your sight, you'll have your *familie*. We're here. We always will be."

The entire household again descended into silence. Tension rippled through the air as everyone waited for Noem's answer.

Pressing out a sigh, Noem rubbed his eyes. "You're right. If there's a chance I can be healed, I'll do what the doctors recommend."

"*Ach*, praise *Gott*." Lavinia was unable to hold back any longer, and her fragile composure snapped. She choked on an unbidden sob.

Brow furrowing into deep lines, Noem held out his hands, seeking hers. "*Liebste*, my dearest, please don't cry." His blind gaze moved randomly, attempting to focus.

"I can't help it." She wept with relief. "I was afraid you'd say *nein*." A shiver shook her, and no more words came. At the end of her endurance, she barely had the strength to stand.

His strong fingers closed around hers. "For you, the answer is always *ja*."

Cheeks wet with salty tears, she drew a shaky breath. "Promise?"

Cocking his head, Noem forced a wry grin. "You'll not be rid of me that easily."

Pulse skipping a beat, Lavinia welcomed the simple awareness of her *ehmann*'s hands clasping hers. She knew then that she loved him, deeply and truly. His kindness. His smile. The way he'd brushed her hair. And the way he'd kissed her, gently and without demand. When they'd wed, he'd lifted the burden of fear and uncertainty off her shoulders. He'd provided a home and hearth to make them comfortable. And to keep them safe.

A complete and perfect peace filled her. Her fear evaporated, for she knew the grace and glory of their beloved savior to be absolute.

Noem's future—their future—was in the Lord's hands.

And whatever *Gott* had planned for them, they would face together.

Epilogue

A few years later...

The sound of a crying infant shattered Lavinia's peaceful sleep. Groggy and half-aware, she blinked her eyes open. "*Ach*, the *boppli*," she murmured, pushing herself up on her elbows.

Beside her, Noem swung his legs over the edge of the mattress. "I'll look after him. The doctor said you're to rest." Yawning, he pulled his robe over his pajamas before padding on bare feet to her side of the bed. Bending over the bassinet, he scooped up a swaddled newborn. "There, there, little man. *Dat*'s got you."

Marveling at the confidence with which he handled the tiny bundle, Lavinia gave him a look from head to toe. "You've got quite the touch with him."

A wide grin suffused his face. His blond

curls stuck out, giving him a comical look. "Well, he is a *daadi*'s *boi*." He placed a quick kiss on the *boppli*'s forehead. "Nathan Gabriel James Witzel."

Lavinia couldn't help smiling. The sight of her *ehmann* holding their first *kind* filled her heart with a bliss she couldn't begin to describe. They'd named their firstborn in honor of their fathers—as well as the man who'd brought them together, Bishop James Graber.

Gaze shining with pride, he sat on the edge of the bed. "I still can't believe he's ours."

"Well, he is. And there's no sending him back to the cabbage patch." Laughing, she glanced toward the nearby window. At such an early hour the rest of the *kinder* were still tucked into their beds. Penelope, Sophie and Jesse all slept soundly. Peeking through the curtains, a golden-hued light etched the edges of the earth. The new day *Gott* had promised would soon burst forth into glorious light and warmth.

Noem laid the *boppli* in her arms. "I wouldn't give him back for all the gold in Solomon's Temple."

Shifting the soft flannel blanket aside, Lavinia studied her little one's face. Snug in her embrace, the infant dropped back into a doze.

Eyes going teary, she recalled the first time

she'd felt a flutter deep inside her womb. There was no mistaking the sensation. She'd known then and there she was with child. Suspicion soon blossomed into delight when the midwife confirmed she and Noem were going to be parents. In time, she'd delivered a healthy *boi*, at home and without complications.

Now two weeks old, Nathan was quite a handful. Robust, he had pink cheeks and chubby little arms and legs. Born with a mop of blond hair, he was the spitting image of his *daed*. With no jealousy over the new arrival, Sophie and Penelope doted over him. Jesse, now an active and engaging toddler, couldn't wait for Nathan to be old enough to wrestle.

Throat squeezing tight, a single tear trekked down her cheek. And then another.

The Lord has given me everything I've prayed for...and so much more.

Noem saw her tears, and concern shadowed his expression. "Is something wrong?"

"Nein," she sniffed. "I'm just happy."

He chuffed with amusement. "I'll never understand women. You're happy, but you cry."

Lifting her gaze, Lavinia searched his face. His cheeks and chin were heavily bearded, his eyes were clear and a mane of loose curls gone awry circled his head. No one looking at him would ever guess he'd gone through a terrible ordeal—one that had threatened to steal away not only his sight but also his life. Thankfully, he'd had a skilled team of caregivers. The tumor that had blinded him was successfully removed and was not cancerous. After a few months of healing, his vision had returned. His stutter, too, had completely vanished. And during Noem's recovery, Gabriel had stepped up to help manage the buggy shop until Noem was able to return.

In a move that surprised no one, Gabriel had also asked Wanetta Graff to marry him. Accepting his proposal, Wanetta had sold her boardinghouse. Deciding to stay nearby, the couple renovated the old *dawdy haus*, turning it into a comfy little nest. As close as two peas in a pod, they were content. And having them living nearby worked well. The older couple was always willing to lend a hand with the *youngies*. Wanetta's *kinder* and *enkelkinder* had also added many new faces to their extended household.

To accommodate their own growing *familie*, Noem had also kept his promise. Instead of moving, they'd knocked down a few walls and added more rooms to the home he and Callie had grown up in. Half old and half new, the house was a seamless blend of past, present and future. Now that they had made it their own, it was perfect in every way.

"My tears are happy ones," she explained, wiping the moisture off her cheeks.

His gaze searched hers. "Are you truly content?"

"What I feel for you—and our *kinder*—I wish I had the words to help you understand. It's more than contentment. It's serenity. My heart is so full of love for our *familie*."

"Your words fill me with joy," he said, giving her and their adorable *sohn* a tender look. "I know I'll never be Josiah—"

Shaking her head, she brushed her fingers across his face. "Josiah will always have his place. But I've tucked his memory away and closed the box on our past. My soul may belong to *Gott*, but my heart is yours."

Catching her hand, Noem kissed the tips of her fingers. "I never thought there would be a place for me. Say it again. Please. Say you love me."

Smiling, Lavinia tilted her head and offered her lips. She'd never get enough of his kisses. "I do," she murmured, speaking with true devotion. "Always and forever."

She meant it, too. Their life together hadn't started easily. But with faith, prayer and determination they'd made it through. The Lord, with His perfect wisdom and timing, knew exactly what He was doing when He'd brought them together.

And what *Gott* hath joined, no man would put asunder.

Ever.

* * * * *

Dear Reader,

Welcome back to Humble, Wisconsin! I am so glad you have decided to make another trip into town.

The Amish Bachelor's Bride is Lavinia and Noem's story. You may remember meeting Lavinia in *Finding Her Amish Home*. She is Abram Mueller's youngest sister. She was married to Josiah Simmons and had a daughter.

Unfortunately, things have not gone well for her. Not only has she lost her husband, but Lavinia has also discovered Josiah had a shocking secret—one that threatens the very roof over her head. Desperate, Lavinia impulsively accepts bachelor Noem Witzel's proposal. Having just lost his sister to a tragic illness, Noem has taken on the care of his young niece and nephew. What starts as a marriage of convenience soon turns to more as Lavinia and Noem rekindle their childhood friendship. Though their journey to happiness is a rocky one, they will both discover their faith and reliance on the Lord will get them through the hardest of times.

What did you think of Noem and Lavinia's story? I love hearing from readers and would be interested to know your thoughts!

If you'd like to keep up with my future releases, you can sign up for my blog and or newsletter at www.pameladesmondwright.com. While you're there, drop me an email. If you prefer snail mail, I can be reached at PO Box 165, Texico, NM 88135-0165.

Sending love and light!
Pamela Desmond Wright

Get 4 FREE REWARDS!

We'll send you 2 FREE Books plus 2 FREE Mystery Gifts.

FREE
Value Over
$20

Both the **Harlequin® Special Edition** and **Harlequin® Heartwarming™** series feature compelling novels filled with stories of love and strength where the bonds of friendship, family and community unite.

YES! Please send me 2 FREE novels from the Harlequin Special Edition or Harlequin Heartwarming series and my 2 FREE gifts (gifts are worth about $10 retail). After receiving them, if I don't wish to receive any more books, I can return the shipping statement marked "cancel." If I don't cancel, I will receive 6 brand-new Harlequin Special Edition books every month and be billed just $5.49 each in the U.S. or $6.24 each in Canada, a savings of at least 12% off the cover price, or 4 brand-new Harlequin Heartwarming Larger-Print books every month and be billed just $6.24 each in the U.S. or $6.74 each in Canada, a savings of at least 19% off the cover price. It's quite a bargain! Shipping and handling is just 50¢ per book in the U.S. and $1.25 per book in Canada.* I understand that accepting the 2 free books and gifts places me under no obligation to buy anything. I can always return a shipment and cancel at any time by calling the number below. The free books and gifts are mine to keep no matter what I decide.

Choose one: ☐ **Harlequin Special Edition**
(235/335 HDN GRJV) ☐ **Harlequin Heartwarming Larger-Print**
(161/361 HDN GRJV)

Name (please print)

Address   Apt. #

City   State/Province   Zip/Postal Code

Email: Please check this box ☐ if you would like to receive newsletters and promotional emails from Harlequin Enterprises ULC and its affiliates. You can unsubscribe anytime.

Mail to the **Harlequin Reader Service:**
IN U.S.A.: P.O. Box 1341, Buffalo, NY 14240-8531
IN CANADA: P.O. Box 603, Fort Erie, Ontario L2A 5X3

Want to try 2 free books from another series! Call 1-800-873-8635 or visit www.ReaderService.com.

HSEHW22R3

COUNTRY LEGACY COLLECTION

EMMETT
Diana Palmer

COURTED BY THE COWBOY

THE RANCHER AND THE BABY
Marie Ferrarella

Cowboys, adventure and romance await you in this new collection! Enjoy superb reading all year long with books by bestselling authors like Diana Palmer, Sasha Summers and Marie Ferrarella!

YES! Please send me the **Country Legacy Collection!** This collection begins with 3 FREE books and 2 FREE gifts in the first shipment. Along with my 3 free books, I'll also get 3 more books from the **Country Legacy Collection**, which I may either return and owe nothing or keep for the low price of $24.60 U.S./$28.12 CDN each plus $2.99 U.S./$7.49 CDN for shipping and handling per shipment*. If I decide to continue, about once a month for 8 months, I will get 6 or 7 more books but will only pay for 4. That means 2 or 3 books in every shipment will be FREE! If I decide to keep the entire collection, I'll have paid for only 32 books because 19 are FREE! I understand that accepting the 3 free books and gifts places me under no obligation to buy anything. I can always return a shipment and cancel at any time. My free books and gifts are mine to keep no matter what I decide.

☐ 275 HCK 1939   ☐ 475 HCK 1939

Name (please print)

Address   Apt. #

City   State/Province   Zip/Postal Code

> Mail to the **Harlequin Reader Service:**
> **IN U.S.A.:** P.O. Box 1341, Buffalo, NY 14240-8571
> **IN CANADA:** P.O. Box 603, Fort Erie, Ontario L2A 5X3